The E-mail Mystery

Nancy p̲a̲i̲d̲ t̲h̲e̲ b̲i̲l̲l̲ a̲n̲d̲ l̲o̲o̲k̲e̲d̲ f̲o̲r̲ B̲y̲r̲o̲n̲ o̲n̲ h̲e̲r̲ w̲a̲y̲ out
of the ca   fore
she left a   but
he was r   I'll
see him

Nancy l   rose
she had   uter
expert. S   the
deserted   the
feeling   ced
back, th

Without   d.

Nancy s   uld
scream   and
Nancy s

Nancy Drew
Mystery Stories

Available from MINSTREL Books

NANCY DREW® 144

THE E-MAIL MYSTERY

CAROLYN KEENE

A MINSTREL® BOOK

Published by POCKET BOOKS
New York   London   Toronto   Sydney   Tokyo   Singapore

A MINSTREL PAPERBACK *Original*

A Minstrel Book published by
POCKET BOOKS, a division of Simon & Schuster Inc.
1230 Avenue of the Americas, New York, NY 10020

Copyright © 1998 by Simon & Schuster Inc.
Produced by Mega-Books, Inc.

ISBN: 0-671-00121-3

First Minstrel Books printing August 1998

10 9 8 7 6 5 4 3 2 1

NANCY DREW, NANCY DREW MYSTERY STORIES, A MINSTREL BOOK and colophon are registered trademarks of Simon & Schuster Inc.

Cover art by Ernie Norcia

Printed in the U.S.A.

Contents

THE E-MAIL MYSTERY

1

A Puzzling Coincidence

Nancy Drew woke up with the sun, her blue eyes sparkling. "Summer vacation, at last!" she breathed. She jumped out of bed and put on gym shorts and her favorite blue T-shirt.

Nancy slipped into well-cushioned running shoes and attached a yellow portable cassette player to her waistband. She pulled a terry-cloth sweatband over her long reddish blond hair and left her bedroom. She heard the shower running down the hall and knew her father was awake and getting ready for a busy day at his law office.

Before Nancy made it down the stairs, the phone rang. She raced back up the stairs and picked up the hall phone on the second ring.

"Is Carson Drew there?" a frantic-sounding male

voice asked on the other end of the line. "This is Bob Jamison—I'm a client of his. I have to speak to him right away."

"No, I'm sorry. He's not available right now," Nancy said. "I'll be glad to take a message, though."

She heard a click at the end of the line and realized that the caller had hung up abruptly.

"I wonder why he was in such a hurry," Nancy said as she hung up. She jotted a note to her father on the pad beside the phone. Then she headed out into the early morning air, closing the front door behind her.

Before she started her run, Nancy stretched out her muscles, using the front steps as a kind of gym bar. She maintained an easy pace as she ran around River Heights Park, listening to her favorite tape and greeting the other early morning runners with a smile. She breathed deeply, her skin glowing from the fresh air and the exertion.

Nancy hummed along with the music in her earphones, thinking about what a lovely summer it was going to be. She planned to spend the first few weeks in River Heights, visiting friends she didn't get to see enough of during the year, including her friend Bess Marvin.

Then Nancy was going to join her friend George Fayne, who was Bess's cousin, to do some sailing up in Bridgehaven. George, who was teaching sailing at the nearby marina, had invited Nancy to come for a visit. Nancy was looking forward to the trip.

Nearly at the end of her run, Nancy turned up the driveway to the house where she lived with her father and their longtime housekeeper, Hannah Gruen. Hannah had been like a mother to Nancy since Nancy's mother had died, when she was three.

Nancy slowed to a walk, then stretched out again. Next she ran up the stairs two at a time, jumped into the shower, and dressed for the day in jeans and a colorful cotton shirt.

By the time Nancy got downstairs, her father, attorney Carson Drew, was seated at the kitchen table, looking at some legal papers. He was so engrossed in his reading that he barely noticed the steaming pile of pancakes sitting in front of him. Hannah was at the stove making another batch and greeted Nancy with a smile.

"How was your run, dear?" Hannah asked.

"Great! I went all the way around the park. It's gorgeous outside. Not a cloud in the sky, and flowers are blooming everywhere."

Nancy's stomach rumbled as she sniffed the rich aroma in the air. "What smells so good?" she asked as she took a seat across from her father.

"Your favorite breakfast," Hannah said. She handed Nancy a plate of pancakes.

"Mmm. Your blueberry pancakes are always super, Hannah, but these look really delicious!"

3

Nancy turned to her father, who usually echoed such compliments to Hannah. Today, however, Mr. Drew was silent.

Hannah raised her eyebrows at Nancy. "It's those fresh blueberries," she said. "You know I always like to get the first fruits of the season."

Still not a word out of Carson Drew. Nancy grinned, then said, "Of course, it's the motor oil on top that makes them taste so good. Don't you agree, Dad?"

"Yes, of course, Nancy," Mr. Drew replied.

Nancy and Hannah laughed out loud.

"What?" Mr. Drew asked innocently. "Did I say something funny?"

"Not really, Dad," Nancy said. "It's just that you're not all here."

"I'm sorry, Nancy, Hannah—I guess I'm a little preoccupied."

"Is something wrong, Dad?" Nancy asked.

"I'm not sure. I've been involved in several cases recently that settled out of court very quickly— much sooner than I would have expected."

Nancy's father was a respected attorney, and he often told Nancy about some of the more interesting details of his cases.

"I thought settling was good," Nancy said. "Doesn't it mean that both sides are happy?"

"Yes," Mr. Drew said, "but some of these cases were settled too quickly. Two of them were settled

4

barely after I'd gotten any information from my client."

"That sounds odd," Nancy said.

"It is a bit odd. People often get better settlements by going to court," Mr. Drew said. He put aside his legal papers and began to attack the stack of pancakes in front of him. "Nancy was right, Hannah. These are delicious. Please pass the motor oil," he added with a grin.

Nancy passed him the jug of maple syrup, smiling at his joke. "I *knew* you were listening. Is there anything that connects all these clients to one another?"

"Two things," Mr. Drew replied. "Williams and Brown represented all the opposition. Also, all these clients have been through a criminal court case in the past."

"Do you think there's something that they're trying to hide by settling quickly and not being in the public eye? Maybe something related to their criminal cases?" Nancy asked.

"I'm not sure," Mr. Drew said. "But these clients did seem unusually scared. They wouldn't even talk to me after they settled. They wouldn't explain what had happened. Some of them are people I've known for years."

"It really sounds as if something funny is going on," Nancy said. "Why are these clients so scared? Are you sure there aren't any connections, other than Williams and Brown, between them? Or the companies they're settling with? Or—"

"Hold on, Nancy," Mr. Drew said with a smile. "All your speculating does give me an idea. I have to devote my time to the Harris embezzlement case, at Central City Savings and Loan. I was wondering if you would be interested in coming in and—"

"Helping out around the office?" Nancy finished the sentence for her father. "I'd be glad to. When do I start?"

"How does today sound?" Mr. Drew answered. "You could put the files related to these cases on disks for long-term storage. You could E-mail some letters and hand-deliver some notarized documents regarding the settlements to Williams and Brown."

"Sounds great," Nancy replied. "This will keep me busy before I go visit George. It'll be great to see Ms. Hanson again. Also, I'll get to meet the new associate, Blaine Warner. And you've got some other new people, right?"

"Yes," her father replied. "There's Henry Yi, our paralegal. He's very bright. And Byron Thomas is our summer law student intern. He's quiet but very thorough in his work. I think you'll like them all. I'll be needing their help on this new Harris case, so you'll be pretty much on your own."

"I may also be able to discover what's going on with all those settled cases while I do the filing, Dad," Nancy said. "I mean, is there one big corporation behind all these cases that doesn't want to be exposed for manufacturing faulty products, or—"

Now it was Carson Drew's turn to laugh. "Nancy, you're always looking for a mystery—whether it's my not talking at breakfast or clients settling their cases early, or—"

Before Mr. Drew could finish his sentence, he was interrupted by the ringing of the telephone. "Who could that be calling this early in the morning?" Mr. Drew wondered out loud. He stood up and walked over to pick up the kitchen phone. "Hello?" he said.

The person on the other end of the line was speaking so loudly that Nancy could hear the words clearly. "Mr. Drew, I've decided to take the settlement," the person said.

"Bob? Is that you?" Nancy's father said. "What's the matter? I thought we—"

"I've made up my mind, and I don't want to go through the whole court thing again. Just take the settlement. Take the settlement!" he yelled. Nancy could hear the click of the receiver as the caller hung up abruptly.

Mr. Drew stared at the receiver for a second before he, too, hung up. "I think you've just found yourself a new case, Nancy."

2

Mysterious Transmissions

"Was that Bob Jamison?" Nancy asked.

"How did you know?" her father asked as he began to gather the legal papers he had been reading.

"I could hear his voice from all the way over here," she replied. "I forgot to tell you that he called really early this morning, just before I went out for my run. You were in the shower, and I told him you weren't available at the moment. He sounded really upset."

"This is disturbing," Carson Drew said. "Bob didn't even give me a chance to ask him why he wanted to settle. He sounded positively frantic."

Hannah started clearing the breakfast table.

Nancy helped her rinse the dishes before putting them in the dishwasher.

"I'm on the case, Dad," Nancy said.

"If you're working in your father's office today," Hannah told Nancy, "you'd better go change out of your jeans."

"Good idea, Hannah," Nancy said. "I'll just be a minute."

"Fine," her father replied. "That way I can look over this file again." He took his papers out of his briefcase and sat down on a comfortable chair in the living room.

Nancy ran upstairs and changed into a light tan spring suit. She put on a white blouse, a gold chain, and added a touch of pale lipstick. "That's better," she said, examining herself in the mirror.

Nancy picked up her suit jacket, grabbed a small leather portfolio, and ran downstairs to meet her father. He smiled at his daughter's quick transformation and packed up his papers in his briefcase.

"'Bye, Hannah," Nancy called out as they opened the front door.

"See you later, you two," she replied from the kitchen. "Stay out of trouble."

"Let's walk this morning, Dad," Nancy said, once they were on the sidewalk. "It's such a beautiful day!"

"Good idea," Mr. Drew replied. "I'm glad I'm not carrying one of my fifty-pound briefcases."

Nancy gazed fondly at her blue Mustang sitting in their driveway. It had been a gift from her father, and she loved that car. But she was looking forward to talking with her father on their way to the office.

Father and daughter walked in silence for a while, enjoying River Heights in early summer: daffodils, hyacinths, and tulips in a riot of yellows, pinks, and purples decorated the front lawns of many of the houses. Rosebushes filled the air with their heady scent.

"Dad," Nancy said as they walked, "if I run into any problems cleaning up your computer files, I can call Bess for advice."

"Bess?" Mr. Drew asked. "I didn't know Bess was a computer whiz."

"You know how she's always loved reading romances?" Nancy asked. "Well, she's just joined an Internet chat group about historical and contemporary romance novels. Being on-line was so interesting to her that she learned all about computers, communications systems, Internet links, Web browsers—all that stuff."

"Bess chatting about romance novels on-line. That's a *novel* idea," Mr. Drew said as they neared the downtown business district where his law offices were located.

"Very funny, Dad," Nancy said with a giggle.

During the conversation, Nancy and her father arrived at the downtown office building that housed his law practice. They entered the lobby and rode the elevator up. Once inside the reception area, Nancy greeted Mr. Drew's longtime legal secretary and personal assistant, Ms. Hanson.

"Nancy, how nice to see you!" Ms. Hanson said as Nancy entered the office with her father. "What a pleasure. Or is it business?"

"A bit of both," Nancy replied, hanging up her suit jacket.

"Nancy's going to clean up all those files on the computer about those cases that settled recently," Mr. Drew explained. "In fact, we got another one this morning—Bob Jamison."

"Bob Jamison!" Ms. Hanson exclaimed. "You just met with him yesterday."

"I know, I know," Mr. Drew said. "He sounded just like the others. He didn't want to go to court again, and he didn't give me a chance to ask him why he wanted to take the settlement so quickly. But as I was saying to Nancy this morning, I can't focus on settled cases now."

"Because of the Harris case, right?" Ms. Hanson said with a knowing nod.

"Exactly," Mr. Drew replied. "It's got us all so busy. That's why I've asked Nancy to come in and help out."

"Well, it's lovely to see you again, Nancy."

Mr. Drew left the reception area and headed into his private office, leaving Nancy and Ms. Hanson alone.

"Boy, another one for the collection," Nancy commented, reading the inscription on the base of a large silver award cup that her father had received from the legal community.

"You bet," Ms. Hanson said. "And you can bet there are a few other law firms that wish they had your father's reputation—and his business."

"Oh, Ms. Hanson, quit cheering for the home team." Nancy turned to see a handsome young man step into the reception area.

"Who's the new assistant?" he asked as he flashed a grin at Nancy.

"Henry Yi, meet Nancy Drew, Carson's daughter," Ms. Hanson said. "She'll be helping out in the office for a week or so."

"Oh, wow, the boss's daughter," Henry said as he shook hands with Nancy. "Better watch my step. Nice to meet you. I'm the chief cook and bottle washer here—also known as the paralegal." Henry flashed his attractive grin again.

"Nice to meet you, too, Henry," Nancy replied, gently removing her hand from his.

Henry turned quickly as another young man walked past them in the hallway. "Byron, come here," he called out to the young man, who was carrying a stack of files in his arms.

"Nancy, this is Byron Thomas, our summer law school intern," Henry said. "Oh, well, I guess you can't shake hands right now, can you, Byron? This is Nancy, Mr. Drew's daughter. You two will probably be seeing a lot of each other in the library. She's helping out here for the next few days."

"Hello," Nancy said, smiling at Byron. He nodded shyly and continued silently up the hallway to the law library.

"So, what will you be working on, Nancy?" Henry turned back to Nancy.

"Just clearing some old files off the computer, so my dad can keep all you guys at work on his new case," Nancy said.

"All which guys?" came a strong, female voice from the hallway. A tall woman walked into the reception room. "Are you flirting again, Henry? I thought I gave you some research to do." Nancy wondered if the woman was teasing Henry, or if she was serious.

"Yes, Ms. Warner, I was just on my way," Henry replied quickly. "And, I'd like you to meet—"

"That's all right, Henry," Ms. Hanson said, shooing him out. "I'll take care of the introductions. Blaine, this is Nancy Drew, Carson's daughter. I'm sure you've heard about her."

"Ah, Sherlock Holmes Junior. Yes, indeed, Ms. Drew, I've heard a lot about you. Your father has told me about some of your exploits as a junior detective."

Nancy noticed that Blaine's tone of voice was formal. Her manner wasn't exactly cold, but it certainly wasn't warm, Nancy thought as Blaine held out a hand to shake Nancy's.

13

"And I've heard a lot about you," Nancy said, shaking hands with a firm grip. "My dad has said he hopes you'll be a role model for me, so that I'll follow in both your footsteps and become a lawyer."

Blaine's comment about Nancy's being a junior detective bothered Nancy a little, but she decided not to let it get to her. Maybe it's Blaine's attempt at humor, she thought.

"I see," Blaine said. "And to what do we owe the honor of your presence in the office today?"

"I'm just helping with some filing so my dad can concentrate on the Harris case," Nancy replied. "I'll be working here for only a few days before I go visit my friend George and do some sailing. I'm really looking forward to it."

"Well, right now you can look forward to this," her father said as he entered from his office with a stack of files in his arms. "Oh, good morning, Blaine. I'm glad you two have had a chance to meet. And if you wouldn't mind, Blaine, I'd like to go over some of these files on the Harris case now."

"Right away, Mr. Drew," Blaine replied. Without excusing herself, Blaine followed Carson into his private office and closed the door behind them.

Ms. Hanson smiled at Nancy. "You'll need a temporary password to get into the computer system, Nancy." She handed Nancy a piece of paper with some information written on it. "Here it is."

"Thanks, Ms. Hanson. I'd better get started."

Nancy carried the stack of files her father had given her into the law library.

Mr. Drew's office law library was lined with oak bookshelves, which were filled with heavy volumes of law books and old case files.

Since most legal research was now conducted online, Mr. Drew had turned his law library into the office computer center, too. In the center of the room was a long oak table with several stations on either side. Each station had a pull-out keyboard tray under a monitor, and special file boxes for storing floppy disks.

Nancy chose a computer station, turned on the machine, and waited for it to boot up. She looked through the first file of papers her father had given her and saw they were the papers for Bob Jamison, the man who had called to ask her father to settle his case earlier that morning. She noted that he had come in to see her father for the first time just the week before.

I wonder what made him want to settle so soon? Nancy asked herself as she began the time-consuming process of searching through all the memos and documents related to the settled case. Then she copied the files off the computer and onto floppy disks for storage. Finally she cleared the files off the main computer system.

It was a tedious job that required a lot of cross-checking to make sure she hadn't missed any files. Often, the documents were not clearly labeled, and

15

Nancy found she had to read a number of letters and memos to make sure they did relate to the case.

She learned that Bob Jamison was a building contractor injured in a fall from a faulty ladder. He had been offered a low settlement by the manufacturer's insurance company.

When she had transferred all the Jamison files to storage disks, she read about more people who had settled cases.

Jeannette King was a bank manager. She had sued her employer because she'd claimed she had been passed over for a promotion that she felt she deserved. The new job had been given to a male employee with much less experience. She'd dropped the suit and accepted a raise in pay as a settlement. James Fox was a local councilman, who was well-known as a crime fighter. He had agreed to settle a case in which he had been injured in a car accident. Harriet Wasser was a landlord who'd agreed to sell a building to her tenants rather than confront them in court.

Nancy couldn't find any notes about the previous criminal cases her father had said he had handled for these clients. She wrote the four names down on a list and put it in her portfolio.

Nancy decided that when she had a break in her file-copying work she would look up the old criminal case files in the storage area.

After a couple of hours Nancy interrupted her file copying to do something a little different. The stacks of material her father had given her included copies of the settlement letters prepared by her father and his legal assistants. Nancy's father had asked her to transmit these letters via E-mail to Williams & Brown, the law firm representing the opposition in all the recently settled cases. Original copies of the letters and other documents would have to be hand-delivered later.

Nancy exited the directory listing the settled cases and returned to the main computer directory. She entered the "virtual mailroom." There she addressed the copies of the settlement documents to the phone number listed for Williams & Brown and dialed them on the modem.

She heard the familiar whirring and whine as the computer modem dialed the computer at the other end of the line, waiting until a metallic click confirmed that she had a connection. Then Nancy pressed the Send key to transmit the files.

Nancy read through the information on the screen as it was being sent through the phone lines to the other office: law firm name; phone number; address; name of her father's client and Williams & Brown's client.

When the transmissions were complete, Nancy returned to her file copying. She pressed the key to view one of the files.

Suddenly Nancy was looking at an E-mail log file with a list of all E-mail sent regarding the settled cases. She saw several transmissions to the same computer phone number she had just E-mailed, that of Williams & Brown.

Nancy furrowed her brow. "That's odd," she muttered to herself. What was disturbing her about the information in this file? Then her eyes opened wide. The dates! She checked to see if her memory was correct. Bob Jamison had come in the past week, and on that same day someone in her father's office had transmitted E-mail to someone at Williams & Brown.

Nancy checked the dates of the first visits of all the clients. In each case, someone had transmitted E-mail to Williams & Brown on the first day the case had been received.

Nancy sat back in her chair and thought for a second. She had learned a lot about the law over the years from her father. She knew that anything that a client told a lawyer was called privileged information. That meant the information was secret. Was someone from her father's office sending privileged information to help Williams & Brown?

3

An Unexpected Encounter

Don't jump to conclusions, Nancy scolded herself. She knew attorneys on both sides of a case must share information with each other at some point during a trial.

Nancy looked up at the rustle of papers and saw that Byron Thomas, the intern, had sat down at one of the other computer stations in the library. He popped a floppy disk into his computer, looked up at Nancy, then quickly back at his computer screen.

Nancy stood up to stretch her legs, then walked over to Byron. "Excuse me. Do you mind if I ask you a question?" she said.

"Go ahead," he replied. Nancy noticed that he had put some handwritten papers inside one of the

19

heavy law books sitting on the desk next to the computer. "What is it?" he asked. He did not look up at her as he continued to type on the computer keyboard.

"You're a law student, right?" Nancy asked. "So, maybe you know the answer to this one. When does one lawyer have to share information about his case with the other side?"

Byron continued tapping away at the keyboard as he answered Nancy's question. "It usually doesn't happen until well into the trial, when the judge orders it. Sometimes you have to send a list of documents, or of witnesses who will testify. But that's about it."

"Is there material one lawyer's office would need to send to the opposing attorney's law firm on the first day a client comes into their office?" Nancy persisted.

"The first day?" Byron asked, lifting his eyes from his work for the first time. She noticed he had deep brown eyes behind his tortoise-shell-framed glasses. "Absolutely nothing. Well—maybe just no-tification that you'll be representing the client. But even that usually doesn't go out for a day or two after you've signed an agreement with your client. Why do you ask?"

"Oh, no reason," Nancy said quickly. "I was just curious. I want to learn as much as I can while I'm here."

Maybe it was just a notification letter, she thought to herself. I don't want to blow this out of proportion. She changed the subject. "So, when do you graduate from law school?" she asked.

"Next year, I hope," Byron said, returning to his computer screen.

"It's a lot of work isn't it?" Nancy asked.

"It sure is. And a lot of money, too," Byron said bitterly. "My parents are helping, but even with loans and summer jobs and work-study, I'm barely making it. I had to take last year off to earn money to pay this year's tuition. It's going to take me more than five years to get this law degree."

"You must really love the law to go through all of this," Nancy said.

"It's my parents' idea, really." Byron closed his eyes for a moment and ran his fingers through his hair. "They just want what's best for me, I guess," he said. Nancy thought he didn't sound convinced.

Just then the door to the law library opened, and Nancy's father walked in. "I see you've met Byron."

"Yes," Nancy said. "We were just discussing how hard it is to get through law school."

"I hope you didn't make it sound *too* difficult," Nancy's father said with a twinkle in his eye. "And I'm afraid Byron's going to be jealous of your next assignment, Nancy. I'm sending you out for some fresh air. You'll be seeing enough of each other in this stuffy library for the next few days, anyway."

Carson handed Nancy a manila envelope, stuffed with papers. "Here are some of the signed and notarized settlement documents on those cases. There'll be more to come in the next few days, all for Williams and Brown."

"I already E-mailed them the files you noted in the folders," Nancy said. "In fact, there's something I wanted to ask you about—"

"I'm afraid it'll have to wait until later," Mr. Drew said. "I need you to hand-deliver these documents to their offices as soon as possible. They're waiting for them. Not everything can be done by E-mail," he added with a smile.

"Williams and Brown's offices are located in that new high-rise at the corner of Maple and Grove, right?" Nancy asked her father.

"Right," he replied.

Nancy took the package, said good-bye to Byron, and waved to Ms. Hanson on her way out of the office. She didn't bother to put on her suit jacket, figuring that the day had become even warmer while she was in the office.

Nancy walked through the streets of the old downtown area. She squinted against the reflections of the strong sunlight on the mirrored surface of the new steel-and-glass building in which the Williams & Brown offices were located. Pretty fancy, she thought, as she entered the cool marble lobby, blinking in the sudden darkness.

The central hall of the new building was designed as an atrium, allowing pedestrians to look up and see plants and interior offices high overhead. Nancy walked up to the uniformed lobby guards at the security desk.

"What floor is Williams and Brown?" she asked. "I have to deliver these papers."

"Fifteen, miss. You'll need a pass for the elevator bank." The security guard handed her a sticker with the date on it and "W&B" at the top. She put the sticker on her blouse and headed for the elevator bank marked 11–20. There she stood with a crowd of office workers waiting to go upstairs.

Next to her, two men in business suits were in conversation. "You guys are the best," one of the men said. "I'm impressed with how you manage to settle these cases so early and so advantageously. I'll be sure to recommend you to my colleagues." He patted the other man on the back.

The two men entered the elevator with Nancy, and all three rode up to Williams & Brown. The second man replied, "We're a family firm, you know. My partner's son, John Junior, joined us just last year after he graduated from Walker Law. We all work together for the benefit of our clients. I'm glad you're satisfied."

The elevator doors opened directly into the

plush reception area of Williams & Brown. As the two men walked through, the receptionist called, "Hello, Mr. Williams." Nancy realized she had been in the elevator with one of the partners of the firm. Nancy guessed from their conversation that the other man was from an insurance company.

Nancy walked over to the receptionist and gave her the manila envelope with an explanation of what it was. The receptionist thanked Nancy and assured her that the files would reach the proper people.

Nancy looked around the Williams & Brown office reception area, noting the leather-and-steel couches, the deep carpeting, the elegantly carved mahogany bookcases, and the oil paintings hanging on the walls. Pretty impressive, Nancy thought to herself.

On her way out, Nancy was joined in the elevator waiting area by a handsome young man about Byron Thomas's age, dressed in a carefully tailored suit. His brown hair curled around his collar. He was with an older man, who had just exited from the other partner's private office.

"Well, son," the older man said, "Bill tells me you're doing a great job handling these insurance cases. I'm sure it will benefit the firm as a whole, and it's a big improvement over your performance at Walker Law. I'm proud of you."

"Thanks, Dad," the young man replied smugly. "It's nice to be appreciated."

Nancy kept her mouth shut, but she realized this must be the other partner, John Brown, and his son.

Nancy knew that a trial could be expensive for an insurance company. Williams & Brown could save their insurance company clients a lot of money by getting people to settle out of court. Some of her father's clients had even agreed to settle for very low sums.

As they rode down in the elevator, Nancy's mind raced. Was someone at Williams & Brown getting her father's clients to accept early settlements? Could this young man be involved, hoping to impress his father and the other partner?

"So, where do you want to eat today, Johnny-boy?" the older man asked as the elevator doors opened on the ground floor.

"Don't call me that, Dad, you know I hate it," the young man said, annoyed. "How about the Steak and Ale."

"Yes indeed, John Junior—sir—the Steak and Ale it is. Anything for our rising star." John Brown Sr. smiled affectionately at his son. Nancy faced the front of the elevator and exited ahead of the two men.

Nancy was sure there was something going on, but how were they making it work? And who was behind it? She walked slowly through the lobby of the office building, her head down, deep in thought about how these cases might have been settled early, and about the mysterious E-mail log she had discovered earlier.

"Excuse me," she murmured as she bumped into someone. Looking up, she saw it was Blaine Warner!

4

A Stranger in the Shadows

"Blaine!" Nancy exclaimed. "Hi. I'm just coming from an errand to Williams and Brown. Do you have an appointment there?"

"No. Why would I be going there? I don't have anything to do with Williams and Brown," Blaine said sharply. "And I thought you were supposed to be working in the law library," she added.

"I'm on my way back right now," Nancy said, struggling to hide her annoyance behind a professional demeanor.

"I'm going to lunch," Blaine explained. "I just had to stop at the bank first. The branch is on the other side of the atrium lobby. I'll see you later back at the office. I know you've still got a lot of file copying to get done. Do you think you'll have completed all of it by tomorrow?"

Nancy smiled but wondered why Blaine wanted her out of the office so quickly. "Oh, no," she said. "There really is a lot of it. It's going to take several days, especially if I have to interrupt the computer work to run errands like this one."

Blaine checked her watch. "I guess I'll have to skip the bank, or I'll be late for lunch. I'll see you later." She exited ahead of Nancy and hurried up the street. Nancy saw her enter the same steakhouse where John Brown Sr. and John Brown Jr. had made plans to eat lunch.

What a coincidence, Nancy thought after she grabbed a quick sandwich and continued back to Carson Drew's law firm.

When Nancy arrived at the office, she greeted Ms. Hanson in the reception area, then proceeded to the law library to continue her work. Henry Yi had replaced Byron Thomas at one of the other computer terminals. He looked up as Nancy entered.

"Hi," he said. "Solve any mysteries on your lunch hour?"

"I didn't have time. I ran some papers over to Williams and Brown for my father. Where's Byron?"

"Oh, Blaine has him doing research for her over at the courthouse. I'm just making some notes for her. The poet is great at writing, but I get stuck with all the technical stuff. You know, no law office runs without a great paralegal, and that's me."

Nancy looked down at Henry's elegant script. He was making notes in the margins of his computer printout.

Nancy repeated, "The poet? Do you mean Byron?"

"One and the same," Henry replied. "He's always scribbling away at something. Maybe he's writing love letters." He grinned mischievously up at Nancy.

Nancy decided to change the subject. "You certainly have distinctive handwriting," she said, her eyes drawn to the artistic swoop of his carefully drawn letters.

"Thank you," Henry said "Even though I'm no poet, I'll bet I could pen a few romantic lines myself . . . if the right woman came along."

Nancy rolled her eyes, then went to log on to her computer again. She looked for the password Ms. Hanson had given her that morning, but couldn't find it.

"What are you looking for, Nancy?" Henry asked. "Anything I can help with?"

"Ms. Hanson wrote down a temporary password for me to get into the computer system this morning," Nancy said. "And now I can't seem to find it."

"Oh, I know all the passwords around here," Henry said. "This should work." He tapped on her keyboard.

Nancy looked up at Henry, who was leaning over her shoulder as he typed. "Does everyone know one another's passwords in the office?" Nancy asked.

"Sure," Henry replied. "We're always finishing up work for one another, so we have to be able to access one another's files. It's no big deal."

Henry continued to stand behind Nancy and study the screen as she accessed some files, preparing to copy them onto a floppy disk.

"What are you working on this afternoon?" Henry asked, leaning again over her shoulder.

"Same thing as this morning," Nancy replied. "And I find it a little difficult to concentrate with you hovering over me like that," she said firmly.

"Sorry. I'm always sticking my nose into everything," Henry said. "I'll just mosey on over here and get back to my own work."

Henry walked away. Nancy checked to make sure he was safely back at his own computer terminal before calling up the suspicious computer E-mail log file that showed that someone had sent E-mail to the opposing attorneys on the same dates as the initial client interviews.

Nancy studied the log file carefully, and decided to print out a copy of it so she could check it out later. She thought that perhaps she would ask Bess Marvin for her opinion, too.

I should also show this to Dad and ask him what it means, Nancy thought. As the printer whirred, she decided not to worry her father until she had more information.

"Making hard copies?" Henry asked. "I thought you were just backing up the computer files on floppies."

"Yes, this is just a record of the E-mail transmission log on this case," Nancy said. "I thought I'd add it to the paper file, in case someone wants to check on it later."

"Those are dead cases, Nancy," he said. "No one's ever going to look at them again."

Before Nancy could reply, Byron Thomas rushed into the library and hurried over to the computer station he had been working at before, the one at which Henry now sat.

"Where's my disk?" he asked Henry frantically.

"Relax, Byronic Man, it's right here," Henry replied. "I took it out and put it in a sleeve before I started my work. Not to worry. How was the courthouse?"

Byron grabbed the disk out of Henry's outstretched hand, tucked it inside his folder, and rushed out of the library without answering Henry's question. Nancy looked at Henry, her eyebrows raised.

"Is he always this excitable?" she asked. "He seemed kind of quiet when we were working in here this morning."

"Oh, Byron's just one of those sensitive, artistic

types," Henry replied. "He doesn't like to let anyone in on his big, important secrets."

The secret of how he's paying his law school tuition? Nancy wondered. Could he be the one sending information to Williams & Brown—and are they paying him for it?

The library doors opened again. This time it was Blaine, with the same harried manner Byron had shown a few minutes earlier.

"Where's Byron?" she asked sharply. "He was supposed to look up some information at the courthouse and bring it to me right away. And what are you two doing sitting around talking? You both have work to do, don't you?"

Nancy quietly continued her work, not responding to the angry woman. "Byron was in here a minute ago, Ms. Warner," Henry replied. "I think he just got back from the courthouse and was headed to your office."

"My office is right across the hall, Henry. Why did he stop in here to gab with you and Nancy? Maybe he can explain that to me."

Blaine turned on her heel and left the library, closing the door behind her. Hard.

Nancy shook her head. "What's up with her?"

"She's always pretty tough," Henry said. "You don't get to be the first female editor of the *Law Review* at Walker Law by being a pushover, believe me. But frankly, she seems worse today than I've ever seen her. Do you think she's jealous of you?"

"Jealous of me?" Nancy asked. "What for?"

"Oh, I don't know. She admires your father so much." Henry paused thoughtfully. "I mean, when you're not in the office, she gets all his attention. Maybe when you're around, she feels left out, like a fifth wheel. Maybe she feels threatened."

I'm his daughter, Nancy thought. Blaine's an associate in his law firm. What more attention could she want from him? Nancy frowned. That was something to think about.

"Where's there a phone I can use to make an outside call?" Nancy asked Henry.

"Well, if you don't want to use the one at your computer station, there's one right across the hall, in the conference room next to Blaine's office," Henry replied.

Nancy excused herself and walked over to the empty conference room. It was time to call Bess. Maybe Bess would know how to find out who had sent the mysterious E-mail and what had been transmitted.

Nancy closed the conference room door, which had a smoked-glass window. She walked to the end of the long table in the conference room. She dialed her friend's number.

"Hi, Nancy!" Bess said, her voice reflecting her happiness at hearing from Nancy. "You're lucky. I was just about to go on-line, and I haven't got a separate phone line for my computer yet. All you would've gotten for the next couple of hours was a busy signal."

"A couple of hours? You've really become serious about this Internet thing, haven't you?" Nancy asked.

"It's so interesting. You can find out anything on-line," Bess said excitedly. "So, what's up?"

"I'm helping out at my dad's office," Nancy explained. "In fact, I was calling to pick your brain for some on-line expertise."

"I'd be glad to help out," Bess said.

"I've discovered something strange going on here at the office," Nancy elaborated. "A number of cases have been settling unusually early, and it looks like someone sent E-mail to the opposing attorneys on the very first day each of the cases was received. My dad said all these clients of his wanted to settle right away."

"That does smell rotten," Bess said. "What kind of Internet connection do you have?"

"I made a printout of the file. If you look it over, could you give me more information about it?"

"I'll do my best. Have you told your father about your discovery yet?" Bess asked.

"No, I don't want to worry him at this stage. I only have suspicions. Maybe you can help me get some proof. What are you doing tonight?" Nancy asked. "Can we meet for dinner after I get out of work?"

"Sure," Bess agreed. "Let's go to that new restaurant downtown, the Sacred Cow. It's right next door to a place I've heard a lot about, the Art-Dot-Café."

"Art-Dot-Café?" Nancy said. "What's that?"

"Oh, it's one of these cool new cyber-cappuccino places," Bess explained. "You can drink coffee and chat on the Internet. I heard about it on-line the other day, and I've been dying to go there."

"Okay," Nancy said. "Sounds great. The Sacred Cow it is. Six o'clock sound good to you?"

"Perfect," Bess said. "And now I'm going on-line."

"See you later," Nancy said.

As she hung up the phone, Nancy noticed a shadowy movement beyond the smoked-glass window in the conference room door. Strange, she thought. Someone had been eavesdropping on her phone call!

5

Caught Off Guard

Nancy jumped up, ran around the long table, and threw open the conference room door to catch whoever it was. The hallway was empty, and Ms. Hanson was not in the reception area, so Nancy couldn't ask her if she'd seen anyone. Who had overheard Nancy expressing her suspicions to Bess on the phone? Nancy realized she had gotten so wrapped up in the conversation that she had forgotten to remain alert.

She could see Blaine sitting in her office next door to the conference room, head bent forward over her papers. Byron exited from the copy room and headed for the library, where Nancy saw Henry standing by the door inside. It could have been any of them, Nancy thought to herself. I wonder which one?

Nancy returned to her file-copying work for the rest of the afternoon. At five-thirty, she went in to her father's office to say good night to him, and tell him that she was meeting Bess for dinner.

"Computer problems already?" he asked. "I meant to tell you that you can also ask Henry for help in that area. He's our resident computer whiz."

"It's nothing like that," Nancy assured her father. "We're just getting together. Tell Hannah I'll be home late and she shouldn't worry about me," she added.

"Okay, I will. But you know that won't stop her." Mr. Drew gave his daughter a tired smile. "Have a good time. See you later."

Nancy checked that the printout of the E-mail log file was in her leather portfolio before picking up her suit jacket. On her way out of the door, she said good night to Ms. Hanson.

"Get some rest, Nancy," Ms. Hanson said with a smile. "You look tired."

"I am tired," Nancy replied. "I'm going out with Bess for dinner, but I shouldn't be out too late."

"Please say hello to her for me," Ms. Hanson said. "See you tomorrow."

"I will. See you in the morning," Nancy said, closing the double glass doors to the office behind her. She rode the elevator down to the main floor.

Nancy strolled down the street in the late afternoon sunshine. She was looking forward to spending some time with Bess, even if they would mostly be talking about the world of the Internet.

Nancy's walk took her beyond the downtown business area to the industrial district down by the river. It had undergone a renaissance in the past few years. Trendy restaurants, coffee bars, boutiques, gift shops, and bookstores had sprung up in the converted warehouse area.

Nancy spotted the sign for the Sacred Cow restaurant hanging over a small doorway and made her way toward it. The sign had a whimsical painting of a blue sky with white fluffy clouds and a brown-and-white cow with wings and a halo, playing a lyre.

In the next building was a small coffee bar with the sign Art.Café at the door, just as Bess had told Nancy on the phone.

Bess was waiting inside the Sacred Cow, sitting at a small table next to a large ficus tree by the front window. She was already working on a shrimp cocktail appetizer.

"Hi, Nance," Bess said, jumping up to give her friend a hug. Bess's blond hair shone in the late afternoon sunlight streaming in the window. "Sorry I started without you. I was starved, and I didn't know if you'd have to stay late at the office—or if the bad guys had caught you already."

"No talk about the bad guys yet," Nancy said. "Let's eat."

The two girls ran their eyes down the elaborate menu. Nancy decided on a cool summer salad with grilled chicken, and Bess chose baked stuffed trout with almonds.

The waitress arrived, and the girls placed their orders. "Why do they call this place the Sacred Cow?" Nancy asked the waitress. "There's no beef anywhere on the menu."

"That's the idea," replied their waitress. "In India, cows are viewed as holy. Even the fast-food joints there serve lamb burgers. Not only do Indians not eat beef, but cows are allowed to roam free in the streets, and no one can bother them. I've been told it causes a lot of traffic problems."

"Let's hope you don't let them roam free in this restaurant," Bess said to the waitress with a smile. "Do you serve Indian food here, too?"

"A few dishes," the waitress said, opening a menu in front of them. "See? There's a lamb curry, there's dal, which is a kind of lentil dish, and there's biryani, a fragrant rice dish made with saffron and raisins."

"Oh, that sounds wonderful," Bess said. "Can I get that with my fish?"

"Sure," the waitress said. "I'll bring you a side order."

During the meal, Nancy filled Bess in on her suspicions and described the conversations she had overheard at the Williams & Brown office when she dropped off her father's documents.

"So let me get this straight," Bess said. "You think someone at Williams and Brown is getting information from your father's office about his clients—information to use to settle cases early. That would save their clients money, because the insurance companies who have to pay out court expenses and financial judgments only have to pay out a small settlement award. Did I get that right?" she finished with a loud sigh.

"Exactly," Nancy said. "Plus, it makes Williams and Brown look good. I heard one of the partners congratulating his son for settling some insurance case early. He said it would help the firm and the son's career."

"So he's got a motive," Bess said excitedly.

"But he would need an accomplice inside my father's office to get him the information," Nancy said. "Unless he could access our computer system from outside?"

"First things first," Bess said. "Tell me about the suspects in your father's office."

"There's Byron Thomas, the summer law intern," Nancy said. "He's a law student with lots of debts—and lots of secrets, too. He always seems to be hiding bits of paper or computer disks whenever someone comes near him."

The arrival of the waitress with their plates of food interrupted the girls' conversation for a moment, but as soon as they were left alone, Bess asked Nancy to continue.

"There's Henry Yi. He's a real egomaniac and a busybody, knows everything about everyone. He calls Byron 'the poet,' and says Byron's artistic side is why he's so high-strung. And then there's Blaine Warner, who's my dad's new law associate. My dad has told me that she's a really tough, aggressive lawyer. But for some reason she was hostile toward me all day."

"So, do you think someone at Williams and Brown is paying one of them to E-mail confidential information from your dad's office? What sort of information could they use that way?"

"I'm not sure," Nancy admitted. "It may have to do with each of their prior criminal cases, all of which my dad handled. I'll do some research on that tomorrow. I hate to suspect anyone in my father's office without proof. So, is it possible for someone at Williams and Brown to access files in our computer system from outside, *without* help from someone in my dad's office? Could someone phone our computer and tell it to E-mail something to them so that no one would know about it?"

"I suppose it is," Bess said slowly. "You can send something to a remote computer, if you've got the password to let you on the computer you're trying to access. But how would someone know which files to get? It seems to me that the person would have to have a contact inside your dad's office."

Bess paused thoughtfully. "What kind of computer security system do you have?"

"Well," Nancy said slowly, "there's an antivirus program that comes up automatically when you transfer files."

"No, no, not virus protection—secret passwords, automatic shutoffs, file coding—that sort of thing," Bess explained.

"There's nothing like that," Nancy said. "We all have passwords to get into the system, but they're no secret. Ms. Hanson gave me one when I came into work today, but when I forgot it, Henry told me what it was, so there's nothing secret about them."

"That's very unprofessional," said Bess. "I'm really surprised. Who's the sysop in your dad's office?"

"What's that?" Nancy asked.

"It's short for system operator," Bess explained with a smile. "That's the person in charge of computer operations at a company or organization."

"It's probably Henry," Nancy said. "My father said he's got a background in computers."

"Then it's not surprising that he knows everyone's passwords. Maybe he's the link," Bess said.

Nancy took a last bite of her salad, and Bess picked the final raisin off her plate. The waitress returned to clear their places and bring them dessert menus.

"Oh, nothing for me," Bess said. "I'm stuffed. Maybe just a cup of tea. No, let's go next door and get some cappuccino at Art-Dot-Café, okay, Nancy?"

"That sounds great," Nancy said.

"Just the bill then, thanks," Bess said to the waitress. Then, once the table was clean, she said to Nancy, "Let me see the E-mail transmission log you printed out."

Nancy carefully removed it from her portfolio. "Ah, you see?" Bess pointed to a line on the printout. "This shows who sent the E-mail: MHans."

"Marian Hanson!" Nancy exclaimed. "That can't be! She's worked for my father for years. You know her, Bess. She said to say hi to you when she heard we were having dinner together."

"People change," Bess said.

"I don't believe it," Nancy said. "Besides, it's just not possible. Look at the transmission times. These files were sent after ten o'clock at night, some after midnight. Ms. Hanson doesn't stay in the office that late. Couldn't someone else log on as her, so it would look as if anything transmitted came from her?"

"If the computer security is as lax as you say it is—sure," Bess said. "Anybody could log on as MHans, with her password."

"Henry certainly knew mine, and it's only temporary, so I can work on the system for the next couple of days. I'm sure he knows hers as well," Nancy said. "And he always seems to be hanging around, asking me questions about what I'm doing when I'm trying to work."

"That could be for a lot of reasons, Nancy," Bess said with a twinkle in her eye. "Maybe he likes you."

"Oh, come on, Bess, this is serious," Nancy said.

"Look, Nancy, even if he's not interested in you personally, he might be trying to impress your dad," Bess insisted.

"What about tracking whether the instruction to send the E-mail came from inside the office or outside it? Can you do something like that?"

"I'll be honest, Nancy," Bess said. "I've learned a lot about getting around the Internet, but I'm not sure I have enough expertise to track a computer criminal through cyberspace."

"Well, do you know somebody who could do it?" Nancy persisted.

"I could probably find someone," Bess said. "But this printout won't tell anyone what we need to know, not even a computer expert. It just shows the information from your in-house E-mail system. We'll need to see where the mail was routed, what

the servers were, and discover the real addresses—
and the actual account holders."

"I can't believe how much you've learned recently. You're way over my head," Nancy warned.

"I'm not sure how to access that stuff, anyway,"
Bess continued. "But I'll tell you what. Let me
come into the office with you, and I'll try to dig up
the file information a computer expert would need
to track this E-mail. Then I'll log on to my
computer-users' chat group. We'll be sure to find
some ambitious computer hacker who'll know what
we need to do."

"That sounds like a great idea," Nancy said.
"Why don't you meet me in the office tomorrow
night after work, and you can show me all around
the Internet."

"Let's go to Art-Dot-Café right now," Bess said,
"and I'll give you a quick introductory tour."

While the girls were gathering up their things to
exit the restaurant, Nancy whispered sharply to
Bess, "Look over there. See that woman, sitting
behind that ficus tree next to our table? That's
Blaine Warner."

"Blaine Warner?" Bess whispered back to
Nancy. "The legal eagle from your dad's office? Do
you think she's following you?"

"I didn't notice anyone following me on my way
here," Nancy said. "It might just be a dinner date.
Can you see who she's with?"

"Some cute guy," Bess said, smiling. "Curly

brown hair, nice looking. I guess being a lawyer isn't all bad."

"I can't believe they might have overheard our whole conversation," Nancy said. She pulled Bess toward the restaurant exit. "Let's just slip out, in case she didn't notice me," Nancy said. "I'd rather not make introductions right now."

The two girls quietly moved toward the door of the restaurant and exited into the cool evening. They turned left to walk into the computer coffeehouse called Art.Café. There, standing right in front of them, as if he had been waiting for them, was Byron Thomas!

6

Well-Kept Secrets

"Byron!" Nancy exclaimed. "What are you doing here?"

"Oh, nothing," Byron mumbled. "I, um, was just meeting a friend for coffee."

"Oh, at the Art-Dot-Café?" Bess asked, smiling warmly at the intense young man. "That's just where we're going."

"Byron, this is my friend Bess Marvin," Nancy said. "Bess, this is Byron Thomas, the law intern at my dad's office. Sorry to jump like that, Byron, but you did startle me."

"Nice to meet you, Bess," Byron said, shaking her hand. "I didn't mean to scare you. I, um, just didn't expect to see you down here."

"Me, either," Nancy said. "So, what's this Art-

Dot-Café like, anyway? Bess here has only heard about it on the Internet, and we were going to try it out."

"I'm going to—um—another place, up the street," Byron said quickly. "A few blocks away. Not here. I'll see you tomorrow, Nancy." He hurried up the block.

Nancy and Bess looked after him. "What was that all about?" Bess asked. "River Heights isn't such a small town that you run into two people from your dad's office in one night. Are they working together, maybe? Do you think they're tailing you?"

Nancy laughed. "I can't imagine Byron Thomas and Blaine Warner working together on anything they don't have to. And Blaine was pretty tough on Byron today. Besides, Blaine's still inside the restaurant, and Byron's walking up the block. Who's following me now?"

"Maybe Henry Yi is behind that tree," Bess said with a grin. "Anyway, enough mystery for tonight. Let's go get a cappuccino at Art-Dot-Café."

The two girls entered the small coffee bar. They admired the gleaming espresso machine on the bar, and the gleaming computer monitors stationed at each of the small wrought-iron tables. The computer wires disappeared into holes in the floor, under the tables. The walls were decorated with modern paintings, and soft classical music was being played.

Small groups of two and three people gathered around each screen, laughing and talking over their steaming coffee drinks as they tapped away on their keyboards.

"This is cool," Nancy said.

"It's just like they said it would be on-line. It's absolutely fabulous," Bess said. "I can't wait to tell my friends in the chat group that I actually came here."

Bess and Nancy approached the coffee bar, and ordered mocha cappuccinos with extra cinnamon. When they received their frothy drinks, Bess stirred in two teaspoons of raw light brown sugar, while Nancy dusted the top of hers with cocoa powder.

"Delicious," Nancy said, taking a sip of the chocolaty concoction. "Now, let's find a table and you can show me a thing or two."

"Great," Bess said. They stood for a few minutes drinking their cappuccinos as they waited for a table to open up. Finally a young couple rose from their station and walked toward the exit. Bess and Nancy moved into the space they had vacated.

"Look," Bess said. "The computer's already logged on to one of the Internet services. Let's browse around and look for some interesting chat groups."

Nancy watched as her friend expertly scrolled through the different screens.

"Yikes," Nancy said, as she read the names of some of the chat rooms. "Some of these groups sound scary."

"Yeah," Bess agreed. "Actually, you have to be really careful on-line. You shouldn't give out your home address or phone number, or let anyone know that you'll be out of town on a certain date. Let's log on to my computer users' group."

The monitor in front of them read, "Welcome to the Computer Users' Forum. Warning: Do not give anyone your password or billing information." Below this it scrolled dozens of names with computer-related questions and answers following behind.

"How does this work?" Nancy asked.

"Each person is identified by a screen name, at the left," Bess explained. "Then you type something in here, press the Enter key, and it appears for everyone to read."

"What's that?" Nancy asked, pointing to a strange symbol on the screen: :-)

"Ha!" Bess laughed. "Turn your head to the side and you can see what it is. It's someone smiling. Get it?"

"That's great," Nancy said, laughing.

Nancy watched, fascinated, as the on-line conversation continued in front of her eyes. She read simple questions from novice computer users that even she could answer, and she read complicated questions from computer experts who used words Nancy didn't understand at all.

"Wow," Nancy said. "It seems like all kinds of people use this bulletin board."

"Yeah," Bess agreed. "It's the best forum to learn stuff about computers, from the most basic to the most advanced. That's why I thought we'd find someone here who could answer our questions about tracking your E-mail criminal on-line."

"I see something repeated over and over," Nancy observed. "What does that mean?" She pointed to a line on the screen: Refer to FAQs@uvm.edu

"FAQs is short for 'frequently asked questions,'" Bess explained. "Most new computer users ask the same things over and over, so it's easier to refer them to an answer sheet than reply personally to each one. The rest of the line tells people where to find the list."

"Are only people in River Heights on-line here, or from around the country?" Nancy asked.

"Around the world," Bess answered. "But there are local bulletin boards, too, where we can chat with people only in the neighborhood."

"I think that would make more sense for us," Nancy said.

"Okay," Bess said. "I'll post a notice in the local computer users' newsgroup. If people around here can help us, they'll post a response, and we can check if we got an answer when we meet in the office tomorrow night."

"Wait a sec," Nancy said as Bess's hands flew over the keyboard. "Don't give out any private information, like that the problem is in my dad's office, or even that it's law related. And you said we can't give out our phone numbers. Remember that warning at the top of the screen not to give out your password."

"I know that, Nan. Don't worry," Bess said. "How's this?" she asked, showing Nancy what she was going to post.

Seeking help to track E-mail from one place to another: who sent it, who received it, was it sent in-house or from outside. Please reply <BigB@123.com>

"Perfect," Nancy said. "It doesn't give away anything—except your E-mail address at the end, right?"

"Right," Bess confirmed, using her mouse to move the cursor onto the Send button, and posting the note. "And even if someone can track my E-mail address, there's no way to connect me with your dad's firm."

"All right, that sounds pretty safe. Show me some more of those computer thingies," Nancy requested.

"Sure," Bess said. "I don't need to be on-line to do that. In fact, I printed out a list of them from my on-line computer chat guide. I have it right here.

"Uh-oh," Bess said suddenly, twisting her wrist to glance at her watch. "It's almost nine o'clock.

I've got to run home so I can log on to my chat group, or I'll miss the discussion."

"Can't you leave me the list?" Nancy asked. "I'd really like to see it."

"I'm sorry, Nance," Bess said. "I'm going to need to refer to it tonight. I promise I'll bring it to the office tomorrow evening."

"Great," Nancy said. "I've got to go now, too. I promised my dad I'd be at work early tomorrow. But can't you just relax and log on to your group here?"

"I could, but I won't have my personal screen name or my printer. I like to download stuff sometimes and read it later. I've really got to run."

Bess quickly exited the local computer users' mail group, where she had posted the notice seeking an on-line expert to trace computer E-mail activity, and logged off the machine.

The girls sipped the last of their cappuccinos, long since cold, and started to leave the café. As they walked out, Nancy asked Bess, "Do you think someone will see that note you posted in the local computer users' mail group and send you an answer?"

"Probably," Bess said. "People on-line love to help one another."

"Or hurt one another," Nancy said, thinking of their earlier conversations about dangerous people and places on the Internet.

Blaine Warner was leaving the Sacred Cow next

door at the same time the two girls were coming out of the Art.Café coffee bar. She nodded hello to Nancy, then continued up the street alone.

"That's the woman from your dad's office," Bess whispered. "What happened to her date?"

"I don't know," Nancy said. "Maybe he couldn't take too much of her, either, so he ran out early and left her with the check."

The two girls laughed, and said good night. Then they walked their separate ways home.

The next day Nancy went into the office early. Since she was alone in the library, she decided to research the backgrounds, specifically any criminal cases, of her father's clients who had recently settled claims quickly.

Nancy pulled out her list of the clients' names and scanned the heavy red legal folders where the old cases were stored. "Let's see . . . Bob Jamison . . . James Fox . . . Jeannette King . . . Harriet Wasser . . . here they are."

The first thing Nancy noticed was that the files were all free of dust, even though some of the cases were several years old. Either the janitorial staff here is very thorough, Nancy thought, or someone else looked at these files recently and wiped them off.

Nancy sat down with the thick files and began to flip through the papers inside. As she read she discovered that in each case there was information from a previous criminal case that could possibly harm the client in the current case.

Bob Jamison, the contractor who had been injured falling off a ladder, had had a similar injury from an old car accident. That might cause a problem in the new case, Nancy thought. Jeannette King, the bank manager who had been going to sue for job discrimination, had been wrongly accused of stealing money when she had been a teller. Carson Drew had got her an acquittal, but Nancy thought Ms. King's background might hurt her in the new case, and she probably didn't want to have the old charges brought up again.

James Fox, the councilman with the get-tough-on-crime policy, had a drunken driving conviction that had come out during his previous case. He sure wouldn't want anything like that to come out, Nancy thought. And Harriet Wasser, the landlord who had sold her building to her tenants, had been indicted for not providing heat in the middle of winter.

It sure looks as though all of these people have a reason not to want to go to court again, Nancy thought. I have to talk to them and find out why they're so scared. Maybe someone from Williams & Brown got hold of this information and threatened them with leaking it if they didn't settle quickly.

As Nancy sat there, looking at the files, Henry

walked in. "Good morning," he said cheerily. "What are you doing, Nancy?" he asked. "I thought you were just backing up computer files."

"Well," Nancy said, thinking fast, "I also have to file the paperwork connected with the cases, so I was just studying the old files to see how you like to organize stuff here."

Henry looked at the names on the files and raised his eyebrows. "These are all the same people who are in those cases you're cleaning off the computer, right?" he asked.

"Yes," Nancy replied, closing the files carefully. "The new cases are all civil cases, which my father doesn't usually handle unless he has a history with the client."

"I've got to make some copies for Blaine," Henry said, changing the subject, to Nancy's relief. He left the law library, and Nancy put away the files on the storage shelf. Then she sat down at her computer and began the file-copying work she had started the day before. But her mind was wrapped up in the E-mail mystery.

Nancy didn't hear Blaine Warner enter the library until Blaine was standing right behind her. "Could you make copies of these documents for me?" Blaine asked, slapping down a thick pile of court papers by Nancy's keyboard. "It's Henry's job, but I can't find him anywhere. I need them for a court appearance today."

Nancy was irritated at having her work disturbed and at Blaine's manner, but she picked up the stack of papers. "I just saw Henry a few minutes ago," Nancy said. "He said he had to make some copies for you. But I'll get them started until he shows up." Then she headed for the copy room.

"Drop them in my office, stapled and collated," Blaine called after Nancy.

"Yes, ma'am," Nancy muttered. Blaine could really be annoying, she thought.

Nancy entered the copy room and sighed. Whoever had used it last had left a big mess on the machine. It must have been Henry, Nancy thought. She put down the stack of papers from Blaine on the paper supply shelf, careful to keep them in order, and then began to gather the papers from the top of the copying machine.

Once Nancy had the surface of the machine cleared, she took the first of Blaine's documents and used the staple remover to pull out the heavy-duty staples. Then she placed the stack of papers into the document feeder.

The machine hummed and clicked, but the papers didn't start feeding through the copier. Nancy noticed a light on the control panel and looked at the readout that gave the following operator message: "Remove original from document glass."

Someone must have left something in the copier, Nancy thought. She removed the stack of papers from the document feeder and placed them carefully on the shelf. Then she lifted up the cover to see what was inside.

There, on the glass, was a handwritten list of all the clients whose cases had been settled early—in Henry Yi's distinctive script!

7

Trailed!

Nancy stood open-mouthed, the incriminating list of familiar names in her hand. Then she quickly put the handwritten document back in the copying machine and made a copy for herself. She had just removed the copy from the paper tray and placed it on the shelf next to Blaine's work, when she heard someone enter the room behind her.

"Nancy!" Henry cried, startling her. "Just the person I wanted to see."

"Oh, Henry," Nancy said.

"No, that's a candy bar," he said with a laugh. "But I assure you, I'm just as sweet. I think I left something in here before," he continued.

"You sure did," Nancy said, opening the cover of the copying machine. "I was making some copies for Blaine—because she couldn't find you—and I discovered this in the copier. I recognized your handwriting; it's so unusual. What are you doing with a list of all my father's clients whose cases were settled early?"

Now it was Henry's turn to be startled. Then he smiled, a little too easily, Nancy thought.

"Well, when I found out that's what you were working on, I thought I'd do a little research, just so we'd have something to talk about," Henry said smoothly. "Get to know each other a little better, you know."

Nancy just looked at him, hands on her hips. She realized she'd better hide her copy of his list. She turned her back to Henry and restacked some papers on the shelf. She asked him, "So, what do you think?"

"About what?" Henry asked innocently. Nancy could feel him watching her back.

"The cases," Nancy replied, turning toward him again with several sheets of blank copy paper hiding her copy of Henry's list. "The ones that settled early. The ones on your list." She brushed past Henry to leave the copy room. Nancy headed for the law library, where she had left her leather portfolio beside her computer station.

Henry answered as he followed her up the hallway, his original list in his hand. "Well, it's a little odd they all settled so early, don't you agree?" he asked nervously.

"Yes, I do," Nancy said as she stuffed the papers into her portfolio, her back still to Henry. "And so does my father." She turned around to look at him and noticed that his eyes were glued to her computer screen. *Is he trying to look at my files again?* Nancy wondered.

"I know," Henry replied almost smugly.

Nancy looked at him. *What is this guy up to?* she wondered. "I don't think you started this list after I came to work here. I think you've had it for some time."

"What makes you say that?" Henry asked defensively.

Nancy didn't have a chance to answer, because Blaine came storming into the library at that moment.

"Nancy, Henry, what are the two of you doing standing around talking *again*?" Blaine demanded angrily. "I stopped by the copy room, and saw all my documents sitting on the shelf, Nancy. And really, Henry, you should be doing that work, anyway. I pulled Nancy off her computer filing because I couldn't find you."

"I'm sorry, Ms. Warner," Henry said, putting his handwritten list under a stack of papers next to his computer. "Sorry, Nancy. I didn't realize you were stuck with my work. I'll get on it right away." He quickly exited the computer room, leaving Blaine and Nancy alone.

"And what were you doing in here?" Blaine

asked, glancing at Nancy's computer screen as Henry had a few moments before.

"I just had to put something in my portfolio," Nancy answered. "Henry walked in on me while I was doing your copying, and started up a conversation. I didn't want to be rude, so—"

"Well, sometimes you have to be rude to get your work done," Blaine said coolly.

"And sometimes you have to go out for an early lunch." Blaine and Nancy turned to see Mr. Drew standing in the door of the library. "Would you care to join me, Nancy?"

"I'd love to, Dad," Nancy said, glad to be saved from the confrontation with Blaine. "I've been wanting to ask you some questions about these cases I've been filing for you."

Blaine looked from father to daughter. "I guess I should get a bite to eat myself," she said. "I always get a little testy when I'm tired or hungry." Nancy noticed Blaine tried to smile. "I should probably get Henry to eat something, too. I've been pretty tough on him today. Sorry if I spoke sharply, Nancy."

"That's okay, Blaine. I understand," Nancy said. She picked up her portfolio and exited through the reception area with her father.

"How about the Steak and Ale?" he asked as they waited for the elevator.

"Sure," Nancy said. "That place really is a hot spot."

"What makes you say that?" her father asked with a smile.

"Yesterday when I delivered those documents to Williams and Brown, I heard one of the partners making plans to eat there. And Blaine went there, too," she added as they walked out of the lobby into the bright sunlight.

Nancy and her father walked to the restaurant and settled in a comfortable booth. They scanned the large menus, and when the waiter arrived, both ordered hamburger platters.

"With a side order of onion rings," Mr. Drew added, smiling at Nancy. "I know you love them."

Nancy asked for a green salad with her burger, instead of fries. "I'll be getting enough grease from the onion rings, thank you very much, Dad."

Once they had ordered, Nancy asked her father for a little more background on her growing E-mail mystery. "Tell me about some of the clients that settled so early. Like that guy who called the house yesterday, Bob Jamison. Why was he so scared?"

Mr. Drew smiled at his daughter's intelligent question, but his eyes showed his concern about the cases. "I represented Bob two years ago when he was a victim in a hit-and-run car accident. He came to see me last week, when he got hurt falling off a faulty ladder he'd just bought. But the day after the preliminary interview, the insurance company for the store offered a small settlement, and as you know, Bob called to say he wanted to take it."

"Did he tell you why he decided to settle so early?" Nancy asked.

"No," her father replied, shaking his head. "I tried to call him back yesterday when I got to the office, but he wouldn't take my calls. If he was worried that the old accident might endanger the case, I would have told him otherwise. The opposing attorneys might have tried to make something out of that, but there would be no basis in fact. The injuries were quite different, and they were all carefully documented by the doctors and the hospitals each time. And anything in our preliminary interview is privileged information. But as you said yesterday, some people are intimidated by courts and lawsuits and lawyers, so he might have felt pressured to give in early."

"Pressured by whom?" Nancy wondered aloud. "And with what?" Then the waiter arrived with their food, and Nancy and her father settled into their big hamburgers, sharing a large plate of onion rings. Nancy looked around her at the other lawyers and professionals enjoying their lunches, probably talking business, making deals, discussing cases.

After the meal, while they were having coffee and sharing a piece of apple pie, Nancy decided to tell her dad something about her discovery of the E-mail log file and Henry's list of clients, and ask him what he thought they might mean.

"Dad, when I was copying those files yesterday, I happened to read the E-mail transmission log. Someone in your office sent E-mail to Williams and Brown—on the first day you got each case. And Henry Yi has a handwritten list of all those clients, too," she added. "Did you speak to him about your concerns?"

"No," her father replied. "I haven't talked about this with anyone at the office. But it's not necessarily suspicious that he compiled a list like that," he continued. "I told you, he's the computer expert around the office. He probably was keeping track of settled cases so we'd know what had to be cleared off the main computer system—what you're doing now. And as for the E-mail log file, that could have been notification to Williams and Brown that we would be handling the cases. It doesn't mean anyone sent them information they might use to force a settlement. Besides, who in my office would do such a thing?"

"Well, isn't it a little strange that all of the cases that settled early were handled by the same law firm?" Nancy persisted.

"Williams and Brown usually represents the insurance company interests, so it's not all that surprising they're involved in all these cases," her father replied. "And I know Bill Williams and John Brown—they're solid guys, with a successful law practice. They'd never do anything like try to intimidate my clients. That's against the law, for one thing. They could be disbarred. And they've got a nice family firm over there—"

"I know, I know," Nancy interrupted. "When I was delivering those files to their office yesterday, I overheard Williams saying to an insurance agent that Brown's son had joined the firm when he got out of law school. And then Brown was talking to his son in the elevator about how proud he was of him for saving money for their insurance company clients."

Mr. Drew laughed. "John Brown's always talking about that son of his. He was telling me at the Northeast Legal Convention that John Junior was having trouble at Walker Law. I'm sure his father's glad he turned out to be an asset to the firm."

"Walker Law?" Nancy asked. "Didn't Blaine Warner go there, too?"

"Yes, but she was a superstar, number one in her class," her father replied. "We were lucky to get her."

"Who knows?" Nancy shrugged. "Maybe there's some new associate at Williams and Brown who's hooked up with an expert computer hacker and figured out a way to hack into our computer system and steal passwords and E-mail out sensitive files and—"

Mr. Drew laughed. "I think you've got mystery on the brain, my girl. That sounds far too complicated to me. And I don't think anyone here in my office would be involved in anything underhanded, or send out privileged information via E-mail or any other means."

Nancy had her own suspicions about the people in her father's office, but decided not to tell him until she had more proof.

Nancy settled back in her booth, and picked up her coffee. Her eyes drifted past her father's shoulder—she had been concentrating on him during their conversation—and she nearly fell out of her seat. There was Henry Yi grinning at her from the next booth!

8

Scared Away

"Henry," Nancy squeaked, startling her father.

"My name's not Henry," Mr. Drew said, smiling at his daughter. Then he followed her gaze and turned around to look behind him. "Oh, hi, Henry; hi, Blaine. You were right, Nancy. This is the lawyers' hot spot."

"Hi, Carson," Blaine said warmly. "Hi, Nancy. I decided I was being too hard on everyone, so I offered to take Henry out to lunch."

"And I, of course, graciously—and hungrily—accepted," Henry said, wiping his mouth.

Nancy sat absolutely silent, stunned that both Blaine and Henry might have overheard some or all of the conversation with her father. "Hi, guys," she said weakly. "I guess this is what they mean when they say you never get out of the office. The office comes with you."

"Especially you," Blaine said, talking to Nancy but gazing at Carson Drew. "You live with the boss." She pulled out an envelope of cash to pay the check.

"So, you got to the bank after all," Nancy said. She looked at the thick wad of bills.

"Oh, um, yes, I went after work last night," Blaine said, hastily stuffing the envelope back in her purse.

Nancy's father paid for their lunch, and the foursome picked up their coats and bags, preparing to leave the restaurant.

"Blaine's taking me to court this afternoon," Henry said to Nancy, "so you should have the library to yourself, unless Byron shows up to keep you company."

"I've got a lot of work to keep me busy," she replied.

Back at the office, Carson Drew went into his private office, and Nancy returned to the law library to continue her chores. While she performed the routine tasks, her mind was occupied with questions about the case.

How could Williams & Brown scare her father's clients? They would open themselves up to disbarment if they interfered with another lawyer's client. Besides, Nancy mused, they had to have a contact inside her dad's office—and I know it's not Ms. Hanson, even if her name is on the E-mail.

Checking the door to be sure it was closed and she was alone, Nancy called up the file for Jeannette King. After looking for her phone number at the bank, she dialed.

"River Heights Savings and Loan," a woman's voice said.

"Hello, this is Nancy Drew. May I please speak with Jeannette King?" she said.

"Certainly. May I say what this is in reference to?" the woman asked.

"It's regarding a confidential legal matter," Nancy replied.

There was a pause, and then another woman came on the line. "This is Jeannette King," she said cautiously. "How may I help you?"

"Ms. King, this is Nancy Drew, Carson Drew's daughter. I'm just following up on some of his recent cases, and I wanted to ask you why you settled your case so quickly."

"I'm sorry, Ms. Drew, or whoever you are, I don't discuss legal matters over the phone," Ms. King replied quickly, and hung up.

Okay. I understand her desire for privacy, Nancy thought. Then she dialed the number for James Fox's political office.

"James Fox for Mayor," answered a bright male voice.

"Hello, this is Nancy Drew. May I please speak with Mr. Fox?"

"What is this regarding?" the man asked.

"A recent legal case Mr. Fox decided not to pursue," Nancy replied, reading through his file.

"Hold one moment, please," the man said. Nancy waited, and then he came back on the line. "I'm sorry, the candidate is unavailable at this time. Thank you for calling." The line went dead.

That's two, thought Nancy. She dialed the number for Harriet Wasser.

"Wasser Real Estate," a female voice answered the phone.

"Hello, I'd like to speak with Harriet Wasser, please," Nancy said politely.

"Who may I say is calling?"

"I'm calling from Carson Drew's office," Nancy replied. She could hear voices in the background.

"Harriet, it's someone from that lawyer's office," the woman's voice called out in a muffled tone. Nancy couldn't hear the words of the angry reply. Then the woman spoke into the telephone. "I'm sorry, Ms. Wasser doesn't have any dealings with Mr. Drew's firm at this time." And she hung up.

Oh boy, thought Nancy. This was going to be hard. She called up the file on Bob Jamison, and dialed his phone number.

"Jamison Construction," a pleasant voice answered the phone.

"Hello, I'd like to speak with Bob Jamison, please," she said.

"May I ask what this in reference to?" the voice asked politely.

"I'm calling from Carson Drew's office," she said.

"Hold one moment," the voice said quickly.

An angry man picked up the phone. "Who is this?" he asked.

"Mr. Jamison?" Nancy said. "This is Nancy Drew, Carson Drew's daughter. I'm just following up on some recent cases here in the office and—"

"Look, Ms. Drew, I told your father I wanted to settle this case right away, and that's all I have to say. I don't know what's going on over there, but I won't be dealing with your firm again."

"Mr. Jamison, there must be some misunderstanding. You've had a long professional history with my father, and I'm sure—"

"I'm sure it won't go on, not when I get threatening phone calls whispering about private information from prior cases in your office. Yesterday I was just scared, but today I'm mad. You'd better not call me back, unless you want a new lawsuit on your hands. There are other lawyers in this town, you know." He slammed the phone down.

Nancy sat back, stunned. Someone *had* been threatening her father's clients with information from his old case files. But who? And why?

Nancy decided to look through Carson Drew's personnel files for more background on the suspects. She accessed the administrative directory. She knew Ms. Hanson scanned in job applicants' résumés, as well as any notes from interviews held with prospective lawyers, paralegals, and interns. Nancy scrolled through the long list of files, searching for background information on Henry Yi, Blaine Warner, and Byron Thomas.

After a moment Nancy came upon Byron Thomas's résumé. He had graduated from Marks University with a degree in English literature, and was a student at Barnes Law School. She could see from his employment history that he had taken a year off to earn money for his law school tuition, as he had said.

Next, Nancy found Henry Yi's résumé. He had attended Taft College and taken a specialized course after graduation to become a paralegal. "I guess he must be pretty smart, or my dad wouldn't have hired him," Nancy murmured. "But his résumé's all over the place. It seems as if he didn't—or doesn't—know what he wants to do." In college, Henry studied mathematics, computer programming, political science, English literature, molecular biology and biophysics, and philosophy.

Finally Nancy called up Blaine Warner's impressive résumé. Blaine had attended Walker Law, a very prestigious school, where she had been the first female editor of the *Law Review*. She had won many victories in mock court proceedings, and she had graduated with a perfect grade-point average.

Blaine also had held summer intern positions at some large law offices in the city, but Nancy didn't see any connection to Williams & Brown. "Other than John Brown Junior's going to Walker Law," Nancy said softly. "But it's a big school. They might not even have known each other."

The library door opened, and Nancy quickly returned to the section on the closed cases. Byron Thomas entered, head down, carrying a stack of books and papers. He nodded hello to Nancy and set up at one of the other computer stations.

As they both tapped away at their keyboards, Nancy heard the telltale whine of a modem dialing another computer on the telephone line. She looked up and saw Byron staring back at her. He quickly turned away, then said, "I have to go on-line to use the Lexis-Nexis legal database."

"Oh, I've heard of that," Nancy said. "All law students and lawyers use that for research, right?"

"Yeah," Byron mumbled. He looked at the crumpled papers on his desk and typed away.

"Byron, let me ask you something," Nancy said. "Do you know if the Internet's all connected? When you go on the World Wide Web or use Lexis-Nexis or just send E-mail—are they separate, or are they all linked together?"

"The Internet is one big network of networks," Byron said, still typing.

"What do you mean?" Nancy asked.

Byron paused in his entry and looked up at her. "Well, big organizations have their own computer networks—lots of computers linked together. And each computer in the network has a unique ID number. You can tell what kind of organization a computer is in by the last part of its Internet address—"

"Is that an IP address?" Nancy asked, remembering the term Bess had used.

"That's right," Byron said. "IP stands for Internet Protocol. So, as I was saying, the last part of that name tells you what kind of organization the computer belongs to. For instance, educational institutions, like schools and universities, all end in 'edu.' Government offices, like NASA or the White House, end in 'gov.' Military groups, like the navy or the air force, end in 'mil.' And commercial companies, like television networks or computer manufacturers, end in 'com.'"

"Thanks," Nancy said with a smile. "This is interesting. Then all these networks are linked together, and that makes up the Internet?"

"That's how I understand it," Byron answered. "There are other sub-networks that use other communications protocols. There's UUCP, for Unix-to-Unix Copy Program, and USENET, where the newsgroups are stored, and BITNET, which believe it or not, stands for 'Because It's Time.'

"I think there are also separate networks for banks and private bulletin boards. But they all have to use the phone lines, so I guess they could be connected in some way. You should ask Henry. He's the computer whiz around here."

"You sound like an expert as far as I'm concerned," Nancy said. "Where'd you learn all that stuff about the Internet anyway?"

"Oh, you know, they teach you how to navigate the Net in law school, so you can do legal research on-line, download articles, things like that. You really can find out almost anything over the Internet," he continued. "There's an amazing amount of information available, if you know how to access it. But I'm no expert, really," he concluded.

"Well, you sure seem to know a lot," Nancy said, rising and stretching her legs. "Mind if I look in? I've heard Lexis-Nexis can be really interesting."

As she began to walk toward Byron's machine, he almost jumped out of his chair, and abruptly switched off the computer. Nancy looked at him with alarm.

"Don't you know you should log off before you turn off the computer?" Nancy asked. "Otherwise you can lose data. Look, I didn't mean to interrupt you. I just thought—"

Byron mumbled an excuse, grabbed his papers, popped a floppy disk out of the drive, and rushed out of the library. What's he hiding? Nancy wondered.

Nancy shook her head and sat back down at her computer station. She continued making copies of the files on floppy disk, but opened each one as she copied it, reading through the material that was on the computer screen. Nothing indicated what might have been transmitted to Williams & Brown in the strange E-mail on the settled cases.

Nancy decided to call up the E-mail log file that she had printed out to show Bess, and look it over one more time. Maybe she should look at the office handbook on their E-mail program and see if it gave instructions on how to trace E-mail more precisely.

Nancy looked through the subdirectory where all the files on that case were still stored, but she couldn't find the log file anywhere.

Nancy's eyes opened wide as she scrolled down the screen. The E-mail list was missing!

9

The Vanishing File

"This is serious," Nancy whispered. Had someone discovered her snooping and tried to cover his or her tracks? She went through the directories again to make sure she hadn't missed the file. It was nowhere to be found. Clearly, someone had erased it from the hard drive, hoping to destroy the evidence.

Oh, no, Nancy thought. Bess had said a computer expert would need the original file to find out who sent it, and whether it was sent from inside the office or accessed from outside.

Nancy started to shuffle through the box of floppy disks she used to copy the files from the hard drive. Had she made a backup of the log file when she was copying files yesterday?

Nancy looked at the pile of disks in front of her and groaned. They were only labeled with the case names, not the individual files she had copied. One by one, she began feeding them into the disk drive, calling up the directories, and reading them slowly. Nothing. Nothing. Nothing . . .

"Yes!" Nancy said aloud. "I've got it." Fortunately, when she printed out the list to show to Bess, she had made a backup copy of it on a floppy. Now she made a second backup to be sure she wouldn't lose it.

But who erased the original file from the hard drive? she asked herself. And why? Someone must have figured out that I'm onto them. Now I'm sure it's someone in the office . . . unless someone could *erase* a file over the phone lines, too. I've got to check with Bess and hope she's found us an on-line expert!

At the end of the day Nancy explained to her father that she would be staying late. "Bess is going to show me some things about the Internet," she said. "Not business, just personal stuff. I hope that's okay."

"Of course, that's fine. It's after office hours anyway," her father said, putting on his coat. "We pay a monthly fee for our Internet link, so it doesn't matter how much we use it."

"Is anybody else working late tonight?" Nancy asked.

"I don't think so," her father replied. "Blaine and I both have early court dates tomorrow. You and Bess will have to lock up. And be cautious, Nancy. I've read a few articles about the Internet. I don't want a virus to get into our computer, or have some weirdo track you girls down."

"Thanks for your concern, Dad," Nancy said. "But don't worry. Bess told me all about how to be careful on-line." Nancy smiled. "Besides, I wouldn't give anyone our home address or tele-phone number, anyway—on-line or off-line."

Nancy decided not to tell him about her phone calls to the clients who had settled. He was too tired, and he was concerned about his court ap-pearance the next day.

Nancy walked her father out to the elevator. The car arrived and the door opened to reveal Bess. Mr. Drew gave Bess a quick hug hello. "Have fun, you two," he said, entering the car and pressing the button to go down.

"Hi, Nancy," Bess said, shrugging off her light jacket. "Let's go!"

"First, let's lock the office door and turn out the lights in the reception area," Nancy said. "We're all alone here tonight." She went to the electronic lock panel located next to the heavy double glass doors that separated the reception area from the elevator lobby, and pressed a code on the computer keypad. Then she flicked the wall switch, and Bess mur-mured, "It's kind of spooky in here."

All the office doors in the hallway were closed. The two girls entered the library, where Nancy had left the computer on. The room was dark except for the small halogen lamp at the computer station, which cast a brilliant circle of light on the table. "Bess, I didn't want to say anything in front of my dad, but someone erased that E-mail log file from the hard drive."

"What?" Bess exclaimed. "Then how can we find out who transmitted that E-mail? The printout is helpful, but I'm sure a computer expert will need the file itself to be able to do any sophisticated tracking."

"Well, the good news is I made a backup of the file on a floppy disk. I hope whatever transmission information we need will be on there."

Nancy showed her the disk. "And I made a backup of the backup when I discovered the original was missing!"

"Smart girl," Bess said. Bess settled down at the keyboard, and called up the Internet connection program.

"I found something else today, too," Nancy said, pulling out her copy of Henry's handwritten list that she had discovered in the copy machine. "Look at this."

"Who's got a list of all those settled cases?" Bess asked. "This is a real clue!"

"It might be," Nancy said. "It's in Henry Yi's handwriting. When I confronted him with it, he

81

tried to make it look as though he just wanted something to talk to me about. When I asked my father if he'd spoken to Henry about the settled cases, he said no, and that Henry might keep track of dead cases so he knew what to clear off the computer. But I'm sure it's more than that."

"And Henry's supposed to be the computer whiz around here, right?" Bess said. "Let's change the screen name right now so no one will know who we are or where we're calling from. How about B and N, for Bess and Nancy?" she asked.

"How about N and B, for Nancy and Bess?" said Nancy, joking. Bess grinned, and entered the screen name: B&N.

Bess dialed out on the modem. The girls heard the whine of the computer dialing, and the click telling them they were hooked in. Bess could hardly sit still as she waited to be connected.

"I also called the clients on that list this afternoon," Nancy went on. "Three of them wouldn't talk to me, but one of them implied that he had been threatened with information from this office, and forced to settle early."

"This is turning into a real mystery. Oh, Nancy—we got an answer," Bess suddenly cried. "I checked the local computer users' group after my romance novel chat finished up last night. Someone had already left a reply to the posting we made asking for expert help, when we were at Art-Dot-Café last night!"

"Why didn't you tell me right away?" Nancy asked excitedly.

"I was so shocked when you told me the file was missing, I forgot," Bess explained. "And I didn't want to call you late last night or bother you at the office today. I left the response in my mailbox so you could see it. Look!" Bess's fingers called up her on-line mailbox. Nancy read, "SEEK and Ye Shall FIND. Meet me in the IRC Computer Secrecy Chat Room tomorrow night after 8 P.M. I'll know you by the rose between your teeth."

"Now watch this," Bess said, her fingers tapping away expertly. The girls watched as the screen welcomed them to the Computer Secrecy Chat Room and posted warnings not to give out their company or school's computer system, modem phone numbers, or other identifying information that could be used by computer pirates.

"There must be a lot of experts here, or this information wouldn't be so dangerous," Bess said. "I wouldn't know how to do anything with information like that."

"There must be a lot of *crooks* here, or this information wouldn't be so dangerous," Nancy said. "Are you sure we want to meet this person, even on-line?"

"We haven't said anything about your father's firm or who we are," Bess said. "So we're safe. Let's get some basic information."

"How will we know who this guy is, anyway?" Nancy asked.

"He said he'd know us by the rose between our teeth. Watch this." Bess popped a floppy disk into the drive, called up a file, then pressed Transmit. Several lines scrolled automatically through the entry box, and appeared on the dialogue screen in an intricate pattern that looked like a flower.

"Bess, that's fabulous!" Nancy cried. "You'll have to show me how you did that sometime," Nancy said. "But right now we've got to find this computer expert."

Suddenly a small box appeared in the corner of their screen, reading "INSTANT MESSAGE FROM SEEK."

"What's that?" Nancy asked. "And who's SEEK?"

"We're being IM'd," Bess said. "Remember, in my message I said we were seeking help. I bet this guy is using that name so we'll know it's him. He must have recognized B and N by the rose between our teeth!" She smiled. "Let's see what his message says."

Bess clicked her computer mouse arrow on the box marked Read, and the following words appeared on the screen: "I knew you'd come, lovely rose. How can I be of help to you?"

"This must be the guy who posted in my newsgroup," Bess whispered. "He sounds kind of poetic. What should we tell him?"

"Nothing specific," Nancy cautioned. "I can't let anyone know someone may be stealing information from my dad's computer."

"Let's see," Bess said. "How about this?" And she typed in the reply box: "Can you help us track E-mail activity?"

Nancy and Bess waited a moment, and then SEEK's reply came through: "Of course I can. Where are you?"

"Wait," Nancy said. "You can't tell him that. He'll know the problem is in my dad's office. He can't tell where we're transmitting from right now, can he?"

"No," Bess said. "That's impossible. I changed our screen name to B and N before I logged on, remember?"

"Okay," Nancy said, "but we can't type sensitive information on-line, where anyone could read it. Maybe we could arrange to meet somewhere public, like a coffee shop?"

"Great idea," Bess said, typing away. "He has to be in the area, since I posted in a local newsgroup. Let's see if he's willing to get together in person."

She typed in her message: "Highly confidential problem. Cannot discuss on-line. Can we meet FTF IRL?"

"FTF?" Nancy asked. "IRL? What does all that mean?"

"On-line shorthand for 'face-to-face' and 'in real life,'" Bess explained.

The screen shifted again, and the girls read the incoming message: "The Cyber Space . . . 8 P.M. . . . tomorrow night . . . bring a rose . . . and your disk."

"The Cyber Space?" Nancy asked.

"Oh, I've heard of it." Bess nodded. "It's another computer coffeehouse, like Art-Dot-Café, but it's also a performance and poetry space. You know, where people read their poetry. It's in an old warehouse building, in kind of a deserted area right down by the docks, just a few blocks from where we were last night."

"Sounds good to me," Nancy said. "Let's make a date."

Bess typed in: "Thank you, SEEK. 8 P.M. at The Cyber Space it is."

One final message came back: "ttfn—cul8r."

"Huh?" Nancy said. "What's that mean?"

"T-t-f-n stands for 'ta-ta for now,'" Bess explained.

"Oh, I get the rest now. 'See you later,'" Nancy said. "You're right, Bess. This on-line shorthand stuff is cool."

"All right, Nancy," Bess said. "I hate to type and run, but I've got to get home for my nightly chat group."

"I know, I know," Nancy said. "Romance novelists. Do you meet every night?"

"Yup," Bess said, logging off, taking out her disk

86

and preparing to shut off the computer. "I wouldn't miss it for anything."

"You're in danger of becoming a computer geek," Nancy teased her friend gently.

"Perhaps," Bess replied, tossing her hair over her shoulder. "But a romantic computer geek."

The two girls powered down the machine and turned off the desk lamp.

"This was fun," Nancy said in the darkness, heading for the library door. "You can show me more tomorrow night while we're waiting to meet SEEK at the Cyber Space."

Before Nancy could reach out to touch the handle, the door to the law office library swung open in the darkness!

10

A Spy On-line

"Who's there?" Nancy called out. She backed away quickly and felt around in the darkness for the desk lamp she'd just turned off.

The overhead fluorescents came on, and Nancy and Bess blinked in the sudden light.

"What are you doing here?" Blaine Warner asked angrily, her hand on the wall switch by the door. "You almost gave me a heart attack!"

"Oh, Blaine, thank goodness it's you," Nancy said. "I thought we were alone here tonight. How'd you get in? I locked the outside door."

"I was working on the computer in my office," Blaine replied, "preparing some material for my court date tomorrow morning. And who's this?" she asked, eyeing Bess.

"This is my friend Bess Marvin," Nancy said.

"Hi," Bess said, covering her earlier fright and reaching out to shake hands with Blaine. "Nice to meet you. I was just showing Nancy some computer stuff. You've got a great setup here," she added.

"Indeed." Blaine continued to stare at Bess. "Have we met? You look familiar."

"We saw you last night, when we were coming out of Art-Dot-Café," Bess said cheerily. "Nancy, I've got to run. I don't want to miss my on-line chat group."

"Press the button to the right of the doors in the reception area to open the lock," Nancy said to her friend.

"Okay. See you, Nan." Bess took off for the reception area, and Nancy could hear the click of the automatic locks as her friend exited the office. She started for the door of the library, but Blaine blocked her path.

"Do you always invite friends up to the office?" Blaine asked Nancy, hands on her hips.

"I told my father Bess would be here tonight," Nancy said, a little annoyed at having to explain herself to Blaine. "In fact, I plan to ask him if she can come during the day to work on this file copying with me," she added, thinking fast. "There's a lot of it to do, and as you said earlier, computer work can be very time-consuming, especially if you're careful and thorough. Bess is very skilled, and I could really use the help."

Not only with the computer work, Nancy added to herself, but keeping an eye on you and Henry and Byron.

Nancy reached for the wall switch to turn off the overhead fluorescent lights once more, but Blaine stopped her. "I've got work to do, Nancy. I'll lock up when I go. Careful getting home."

Nancy looked at Blaine, who was already turning on the computer she and Bess had just used. "Isn't the computer in your office networked into the main system?" she asked Blaine, careful to keep any suspicion out of her voice.

Blaine eyed Nancy steadily and replied, "Yes, of course it is. All the computers in the office are networked. But I'll be needing to refer to some of these law books as well, so I thought it would be easier to work in here—if it's any of your business."

Nancy tensed. Had Blaine monitored their conversation with SEEK from her own computer earlier? Could Blaine be SEEK? Was Blaine able to track B&N's movements on-line? There was no way Nancy could answer these questions. "Okay, Blaine," she said. "Good night."

"See you later," Blaine said, echoing SEEK's final message to the girls.

The next morning Carson Drew was not at breakfast. "He went in early," Hannah Gruen told Nancy, offering her a bowl of fresh fruit. "I think

90

he has a court appearance. I missed you last night," she added.

"I got together with Bess again," Nancy said, helping herself to a banana. "She was teaching me about the Internet. In fact, I'm going to ask Dad if she can help with my work at the office."

"I'd be surprised if you got a chance to see him," Hannah said. "I know that new Harris case is taking all his time."

"I *don't* see much of him," Nancy said, looking at the clock. "I've got to get going myself. I've got a lot of work to do, too." Nancy said good-bye to Hannah and headed for the front door.

When she arrived at the office Nancy greeted Ms. Hanson, then went straight to work in the library. After about an hour she heard her father come in. Nancy stood up and stretched. Then she left the library and went to knock at her father's office door.

"Come in," he called. Nancy entered and smiled at her dad. His desk was piled high with folders and papers. "Just got back from court," he said wearily, "and this is what greeted me. I thought the computer was going to usher in the age of the paperless office," he went on. "But by the looks of my desk, you'd never know it."

"Dad, I need to talk to you," Nancy said.

"You're not going to leave me, I hope," her father said seriously.

"Oh, no, Dad, not till the work is finished. What

91

I wanted to ask is if Bess could come in and help me. The work is taking longer than I thought it would, and I don't want to miss my sailing trip with George. If Bess helped, we could finish twice as fast," she concluded. "Bess is really careful, and she's become a computer whiz. You should have seen her last night."

"That's fine, Nancy. I'm sure Bess will be a big help. Blaine told me you two were in here late last night," Mr. Drew said. "She also said that you were on the Internet. She seemed concerned that you might have been careless and allowed a computer virus into our system or an outsider access to our files."

Nancy's eyes opened wide. "She gave us a start last night because I thought the offices were empty. We'd already turned out the lights in the law library when Blaine opened the door. Believe me, we jumped! But how could she know Bess and I had been on the Internet? We just told her we were . . . wait a minute." Nancy thought furiously.

"What?" her father asked.

"As we were leaving, Blaine turned on the computer Bess and I had been using," Nancy said. "Do you think she could track what we had done? We had changed our screen name so no one would know we were calling from here. How could she have known it was us?"

"I don't know," Mr. Drew said. "She told me Byron Thomas is always going on-line as well, so I guess she has some way of tracking our Internet use." Byron! thought Nancy. I wonder if he tracked me and Bess on-line—or if Blaine's really the guilty one, and she's trying to shift the suspicion onto Byron.

"Doesn't Byron have to go on-line to do all the research she asks him to do?" Nancy asked aloud.

"I think Blaine's just trying to keep track of what goes on," Mr. Drew continued. "I explained that it doesn't cost extra to have people on-line after office hours, and that I was sure you and Bess were careful not to compromise our computer security."

"What computer security?" Nancy asked. "Dad, everyone knows everyone else's password here. Your files are available to everyone in the office."

"We have to operate that way," Mr. Drew explained. "Sometimes I need Blaine to follow up on some work, or Ms. Hanson to print out a file, or Byron or Henry to do further research. They all have to be able to access my files."

He looked at Nancy. "You don't still think some hacker is breaking into our system and E-mailing out sensitive information, do you?"

"Something's going on, Dad," Nancy said. "I'm sure of it. I didn't tell you last night, but yesterday I called those clients who had settled early. Three of them cut me off, but Bob Jamison said someone had made him settle. And he implied that the threat was connected to information from your office, maybe from his old case file."

"This is serious, Nancy," Mr. Drew said. "You should have told me right away. I'd better call Bob, and—"

"Maybe you should wait a day or two," Nancy said. "He was pretty angry. I know this could really affect you and your business, Dad, and I'm going to get to the bottom of it. Bess and I are meeting with a computer expert to see if he can help us track the E-mail that was sent on the first day you received those cases."

Nancy's father put his head in his hands. "Please don't say anything yet," Nancy went on. "I'll tell Bess she can come help me tomorrow. I know you've got your hands full with this Harris case, and I should get back to work now." Carson Drew smiled at his daughter as she left his office.

At about noon Nancy decided to go out for a sandwich. She walked to a nearby deli and ordered tuna salad on a roll.

While she was waiting at the counter for her order, she noticed Blaine Warner, seated in a booth with a young man.

Nancy edged toward the far end of the take-out counter, and pretended to examine the tray of Danish pastries. She kept her back to the restaurant area so Blaine couldn't recognize her.

Nancy listened intently over the din of the busy restaurant. She thought she heard her father's name mentioned, and then she overheard the words, "When we were at Walker . . ."

Oh, Nancy said to herself, it's probably an old law school classmate of hers. Then she stopped herself. I've seen him before, though. In the elevator at Williams & Brown. It's John Brown Junior, I'm sure of it. So, they *do* know each other.

Just then Nancy's order came up. Nancy was frustrated that she couldn't overhear more of their conversation, but she was unwilling to let Blaine know she had seen her. Nancy took her sandwich and a can of iced tea, and went back to the office.

Nancy returned to the library and sat down by her computer to eat her sandwich. No sooner had she opened the bag, when the door opened and Henry Yi appeared.

"Take you out to lunch?" he asked, flashing her a friendly grin.

"Thanks, I picked up a sandwich," Nancy replied, pointing to the brown bag on the table. "But let me ask you something, Henry. We never got to finish our conversation the other day."

"Which one?" he asked, leaning toward her.

"The one about those recent cases that were settled early," Nancy went on. "Remember? We were in the copy room and Blaine walked in on us. I really want to know why you had that list of client names. The one I found in the copy machine in your handwriting." She looked at Henry, waiting for his reply.

Henry's expression became serious, and in a low, conspiratorial whisper, he confided in Nancy, "I think someone may be stealing information and using it to settle these cases early. But I can't tell you who I think it is, until I have more evidence."

Nancy was surprised that Henry was thinking along the same lines she was. But she didn't want to let him know that she, too, was investigating a possible crime. She certainly wasn't going to tell him about the E-mail log file, her research into the old criminal cases, her phone calls to the frightened clients, or her seeing Blaine and John Brown Jr. at the coffee shop . . . or her suspicions of Henry himself.

"Really? How horrible," Nancy said. "Have you told my father about your suspicions?"

"Not yet," Henry answered, still speaking softly. He peered over his shoulder to make sure they were alone. "I don't want to get anyone in trouble until I'm sure who's behind it."

"Please let me know as soon as your suspicions are proved," Nancy said, "and I'll go with you to see my father about it."

"That would be great," Henry said with a smile.

This is a little too easy, Nancy thought. What was Henry's real motivation, she wondered. To get ahead with her father, to get closer to her, or to throw suspicion off himself!

11

Hide and SEEK

At the end of the day, Nancy called Bess and told her that her father had agreed that both of them could help with the computer work.

"That's great, Nancy!" Bess exclaimed.

The two girls talked excitedly, anticipating the high-tech "spy" conversation they were going to have with the computer expert called SEEK, and what sophisticated methods he would use to track E-mail through Carson Drew's computer system.

"Let's meet at Art-Dot-Café, since we know where that is," Bess suggested. "Then we can walk over to the Cyber Space together. I can't wait to meet this SEEK guy. He sounds so romantic, telling us to bring a rose." Nancy could hear the excitement in her friend's voice.

"He's probably just some computer nerd," Nancy teased. "You've been reading too many romance novels," she added, laughing.

"Fine, Miss Detective," Bess retorted, "just for that, *you* bring the rose."

"Okay, I will. See you later," Nancy said with a smile. Just as she hung up, Blaine Warner walked in.

"I'll be working late tonight, Nancy," she said. "I won't be going anywhere," she added unnecessarily. "Are you and your friend planning to play around on the computers again?"

Nancy pursed her lips at Blaine's condescending tone. "No," she said, "I'm meeting Bess for coffee, and she and I will be here tomorrow morning. My father said she could come in and help clean out those old files."

"This Harris case is turning into a monster," Blaine went on. "Next week, we'll be bringing in extra legal help, and we'll need all the computer terminals. I hope you'll be done by then, so we'll have room for everyone."

"Well, with Bess's help, I should be able to finish up in another day or two," Nancy said. "Then I'll be out of your way."

She wondered about Blaine's motives for trying to get her out of the office. Nancy left the library while Blaine settled in at one of the computer terminals.

On her way downtown Nancy stopped and bought a single red rose.

Bess was waiting for Nancy in the doorway to the Art.Café. "Nancy," she whispered excitedly, "isn't that your poet guy—Byron what's-his-name?" She pointed inside the café, where Byron was at a computer terminal.

"He looks like he's getting ready to leave," Nancy said. "Let's go into the ladies' room so he doesn't see us."

The two girls slipped into the coffeehouse and made their way to the ladies' room. They peered out from behind the door while Byron paid his bill. When he went into the men's room, they emerged from the ladies' room and went into the main part of the café.

"Can you figure out what he was doing on the computer?" Nancy asked.

"I don't know," Bess said. "Let's take a look." The two girls sat down at the machine Byron had just used. "Look," Bess said. "He was just on-line with someone at the Cyber Space, see? That's their IP address right there."

"Here he comes," Nancy said. "Duck down behind the computer screen so he can't see you."

The two girls peered around the edge of the monitor to see Byron leave the men's room and head out into the street.

"Let's tail him," Nancy said. "I want to find out where he's going."

"What about our date with SEEK at the Cyber Space?" Bess asked.

"We've got plenty of time," Nancy replied. "Let's go."

The two girls trailed Bryon about two blocks to a small café in a rundown building on the waterfront. The sign over the doorway read The Cyber Space Café. Nancy and Bess exchanged a look, then entered behind Byron.

The interior of the building was sleek and modern, much to their surprise. The walls were exposed brick. Pipes and other building materials had been left in plain sight and painted a dazzling silver. Under the low light, brilliant halogen spots illuminated the small round marble-top tables. People, sitting alone and in pairs, hunched over small laptop computers placed at each seating area. On the stage in back, someone was reciting poetry.

Nancy and Bess saw Byron take a disk from his bag, put it in one of the laptops, and begin to type.

"Do you think he could be SEEK?" Bess asked.

"He fits the description," Nancy said. "Let's find out." After she and Bess walked over to his table, Nancy dropped the rose across his keyboard.

"Hello, SEEK," she said. "Fancy meeting you here."

Byron jumped up. "Nancy! W-what are you do-ing here!"

"I thought this was where you suggested we meet," she replied. "Didn't we speak on-line last night?"

"I—I didn't talk to you on-line last night," he replied. "I just came here a few minutes ago. I mean, I just sent in a poem from the computers over at the Art-Dot-Café, and they said I could come over and read it onstage. Out loud and in person, you know? It's open-mike night, see?" he said, gesturing to the person reading poetry in the back of the performance space.

"You mean you aren't SEEK?" Bess said.

"I don't know what you mean," Byron said to Bess. "Is this some sort of joke?"

"Henry told me you were a poet," Nancy inter-rupted. "but I didn't know you were so serious about it."

"I am serious," Byron admitted. "I'm only go-ing to law school to satisfy my parents, so I can support myself in the future—after I pay off all my loans, that is. What I really want to do is write poetry."

"So when you go on-line, it's not to do legal research?" Nancy asked.

"Not always," Byron confessed. "Sometimes I use the office Internet access to work on my Web page. I'm finally beginning to get some serious attention in underground publishing circles. Tonight's just open-mike night," he went on excitedly. "But if they like my stuff, I can have my own reading on Friday. Maybe you and your friend would like to come and hear me?"

"That sounds great," Bess said.

"Let me know if you get it," Nancy said. "You can E-mail me the invitation," she added with a grin.

"Meanwhile, if you're not SEEK, we're supposed to be meeting someone else," Bess said. She picked up the rose Nancy had dropped on Byron's keyboard. "I hope we haven't scared SEEK off. Come on, Nancy, let's get our own table and see what happens."

"See you later, Nancy. Nice to see you again, Bess," Byron said.

The two girls made their way to an empty table and sat down. They ordered cappuccinos and left the rose conspicuously on the front edge of the table. They eyed every patron who entered the café, but no one walked over to them.

"I hope we didn't miss our date with SEEK," Nancy said, looking at her watch.

"It's only a little after eight," Bess said. "Maybe he had to work late or something."

Nancy sipped her cappuccino. "I told my dad about my conversations with his clients yesterday, and he was upset. I hope this SEEK guy can help us find out what's going on."

Bess checked her watch again. "I guess we might as well go on-line while we're waiting." Bess tapped on the keyboard in front of them. She typed: "hi, everybody. BigB here."

Someone typed back: "hi BigB."

"This stuff is so neat!" Nancy exclaimed. "Look at all these sentences scrolling by. How can you understand what they're saying?"

"Take a look at my on-line chat guide," Bess said, pulling the papers out of her purse and handing them to her friend.

Nancy looked down at the papers Bess handed her, and read:

:)	= smile
: D	= big grin
: X	= my lips are sealed
: P	= sticking out tongue
: (	= frown
LOL	= laughing out loud
BTW	= by the way
brb	= be right back
wtg	= way to go!
ttfn	= ta-ta for now!
cul8r	= see you later

"These are great!" Nancy said, grinning. "It's like being able to talk on the page."

"Exactly," Bess said. "You can do almost anything on-line that you can do in person—except meet this **SEEK** guy on time. I have to get home for my on-line group. I guess this meeting is a washout."

"Maybe it was just some kid pretending to know about computers so he could play a trick on us. I'll pay for our cappuccinos," Nancy said. "You go ahead. I don't want you to be late."

"Thanks, Nan," Bess said. She hurried toward the exit. "I'll see you in the morning," she called over her shoulder.

Nancy waved goodbye to her friend, then began to gather together the papers and disks she had brought from the office to show to **SEEK**. Why hadn't he shown up? she wondered. Was he scared off when he saw us talking to Byron?

Nancy looked through her papers and realized Bess had been in such a hurry, she'd left her on-line chat guide behind. I hope she doesn't need it for her on-line meeting tonight, Nancy thought.

Nancy paid the bill and looked for Byron on her way out. She wanted to say good night to him before she left and wish him luck with his poetry reading, but he was nowhere to be seen. Oh, well, she thought, I'll see him tomorrow.

Nancy left the café, carrying her papers and the rose she had brought for **SEEK**. She had gotten only about half a block along the deserted waterfront street, when she began to get the feeling that someone was following her. She glanced back, then hurried along the dark street.

Without warning, someone charged her from behind. Nancy screamed as loud as she could. Before she could scream again, her attacker hit her on the head, and Nancy sank to the ground!

12

A Shocking Discovery

"Nancy!" Bess ran up the darkened street toward her fallen friend. Her arrival probably scared off Nancy's attacker, who took off and disappeared before either girl could get a good look at whoever it was.

"Bess, thank goodness you were here." Nancy held her head. "Why'd you come back?"

"I realized I'd forgotten my on-line chat guide," Bess went on, "and I needed it for the meeting tonight. I was walking back when I saw someone jump you from behind and hit you on the head! Are you okay?"

"I think so," Nancy said. Bess helped her friend to her feet. "I'm not really hurt, just shaken up," she admitted.

"I'm sorry I didn't get here sooner. I ran as fast as I could when I saw you get hit," Bess said. "Did you see who it was?"

"No," Nancy said shakily. "You were coming up the street, Bess. Could you see who it was?"

"No," Bess said. "It's too dark. He looked slim, and taller than you, but I couldn't see his face. Did anyone else come out of the café with you? Maybe someone else saw what happened," Bess persisted.

"No, I was alone," Nancy replied. "I looked for Byron on my way out to say good night, but I couldn't find him. Besides, I was already halfway up the block when I was attacked."

"You don't think Byron's the one who jumped you, do you?" Bess asked, shocked.

"I don't know," Nancy said, "but I doubt it. Byron doesn't seem like the violent type."

"Maybe it was SEEK," Bess said. "Or maybe this SEEK guy set us up. He had to know it was you because you were carrying the rose. This is getting really scary, Nancy. You could've been hurt."

"I'm fine," Nancy insisted. "I bet you're right that my attacker was the same person who called himself SEEK on the computer. Whoever it was knew we were looking for help on the Internet to track E-mail, and set up this meeting to scare us off."

"Well, it's working!" Bess said. "I'm about as

scared as I've ever been. If it wasn't Byron, who do you think it was?"

"It could be any of our suspects," Nancy said, gently rubbing her head where she had been hit. "It could be Byron, because he knew we were here. My father told me that Blaine knew we were on-line last night, so maybe she tracked our conversation with SEEK. Maybe she *is* SEEK! And Henry told me he had a list of those cases because he thought someone was stealing information from my dad's office and using it to settle these cases early. But he didn't want to say any more until he had proof, so I don't know if he's for real or just covering his tracks."

"Did he mention the Williams and Brown connection?" Bess asked.

"No," Nancy replied. "And I didn't tell him about my investigation, either. Henry, Byron, and Blaine are all under suspicion as far as I'm concerned, and they all seem to be trying to throw blame on one another. As soon as we get some real evidence, I'll tell my dad."

Nancy leaned over to brush off her skirt, and noticed a computer disk lying in the street near where she had been attacked. She thumbed through her portfolio carefully, then picked up the disk and showed it to Bess.

"Look, Bess," Nancy whispered. "It's got a Drew law firm label on it."

"It looks like one of the disks you brought from

your dad's office to show this SEEK guy," Bess said. "You probably dropped it when you were knocked down."

"Nope," Nancy said. "All the disks I brought with me are right here in my portfolio. This disk must have been dropped by my attacker."

"Awesome!" Bess exclaimed. "Then this is a real clue. We'll take the disk in tomorrow and check it out."

"This could prove it was an inside job," Nancy said. "And who's behind it."

Bess insisted on walking Nancy to the bus, even though Nancy assured Bess that she was okay. "I can still catch the last half-hour of my on-line meeting," Bess said. "I want to make sure no one jumps you again."

"Remind me I have to give you back your chat guide when we get to my place," Nancy said as they boarded a bus for home. "But I sure am glad you forgot it, or you might not have showed up in time to save my neck."

"Let's not even think about that," Bess said with a shudder. The two girls rode in silence for a few minutes. Finally Bess said, "Forget about my on-line meeting, at least for tonight. After that attack, we'd better get serious about this E-mail mystery. I can always catch up tomorrow night."

"Thanks, Bess," Nancy said, grateful for her friend's help. She thought for a few minutes. "I'm afraid we have to admit that you and I don't have enough expertise to figure out who sent those files or who's been logging on behind us and tracking *our* on-line activities."

"Well," Bess said, "we could go to the computer department at the college and see if someone there could help us."

"We don't have the time. The fact is, I'm not sure how much longer we'll be in my dad's office," Nancy said. "Blaine said they're getting in some temporary employees to help with his new case, and we have to finish up the file-copying work in the next day or two. Without a computer expert we can trust, we have to turn our attention to the suspects at hand."

"Good idea, Nan," Bess said. "I'll help you snoop around when I come in to your dad's office tomorrow."

"Besides," Nancy continued, "it's clear now that even if you could access my father's computer system from outside, the information from those old criminal cases wouldn't be in the system."

"Why not?" Bess asked.

"Because those are dead files. They've all been cleared off the main computer, backed up on floppies, and stored in these red legal files in the law library. And someone's looked at them recently. Someone from my dad's office *has* to be involved," Nancy concluded.

The girls arrived at Nancy's house and were welcomed by Hannah Gruen. "Bess, how nice to see you. I didn't know you planned on coming home with Nancy tonight."

"Hi, Hannah," Bess said warmly. "We didn't plan on it, actually. Here we are."

Nancy put a hand to her head. "Nancy, dear, what's the matter?" Hannah asked with concern. "Did you get hurt?"

"Oh, no, Hannah," Nancy said, dropping her hand and shooting Bess a warning look. "I just have a killer headache. A couple of aspirins, and I'll be fine."

"I'll get them for you right now," Hannah replied as she hurried to the bathroom.

"Are you sure we shouldn't tell Hannah and your dad about what happened tonight?" Bess whispered to Nancy, once Hannah was out of earshot.

"Absolutely not," Nancy whispered back. "Hannah would worry herself to death. And if I tell Dad, he might pull us off the case before we find out who's behind it. I'm afraid he might accuse the wrong person . . . or worse, keep trusting the wrong person."

Hannah returned with the aspirins and a glass of water. "Here you are, dear. You should get some rest, too," she added, looking at Bess.

"I won't be staying long, Hannah," Bess assured her warmly. "Nancy and I just have to go over a few things so I'll be prepared to help out tomorrow," she added honestly.

Bess and Nancy went up to Nancy's room.

"I'm going to do something I haven't done since third grade," Nancy said. She took out an old blue notebook and turned to a clean page. She spoke out loud as she jotted some notes. Bess read over her shoulder.

Clues:

Log file showed MHans transmitted E-mail to Williams & Brown the first day cases received. File was erased from hard drive, but Nancy had printout and backup copy.

Nancy overheard conversations between an insurance rep and Williams about settling cases, which saved Williams & Brown money. Brown complimented his son on how he handled insurance cases.

Someone eavesdropped on Nancy's conference room phone call to Bess, when Nancy talked about her suspicions on the settled cases.

"You didn't tell me about that," Bess said as Nancy scribbled away.

Someone named SEEK answered Bess's posting on local computer users' group. Meeting set up at the Cyber Space, but SEEK didn't show up. Nancy carried rose, and she was attacked.

Computer disk from Carson Drew's office

was discovered where Nancy was attacked. Who left it—Henry, Byron, or Blaine?

Suspects:

Henry Yi: Computer whiz who made hand-written list of clients in the settled cases. Claims someone is stealing information. Is attentive to Nancy—hangs around when she's working. May have overheard Nancy's conversation with her father about the settled cases in the restaurant, when he was in next booth with Blaine Warner.

Blaine Warner: Seems to resent Nancy's presence. Walked into the lobby of Williams & Brown's building when Nancy was there, and went to lunch in the same restaurant with Brown and son. Was at Sacred Cow restaurant when Nancy and Bess made plans to go on-line and in the office the following night when they did.

"Maybe she *is* SEEK," Bess muttered. "Who says it has to be a guy?"

"Good point, Bess," Nancy said as she continued writing.

Blaine and Henry were at Steak & Ale restaurant when Nancy and father discussed the settled cases.

Byron Thomas: Clearly comfortable navigating the Internet. Always hiding papers and computer disks. Bess and Nancy trailed him to the Cyber Space. But he confessed only to writing poetry. Is someone at Williams & Brown paying him money he needs for law school to E-mail sensitive information from the old case files?

"Well, there it is," Nancy said. "The clues, the suspects . . . and tomorrow we'll find out what's on this computer disk."

"Let's sleep on it," Bess said. "I'm ready to sign off."

The next day Bess and Nancy met in the lobby of Carson Drew's office building early in the morning. "How are you feeling, Nan?" Bess asked quietly, concerned for her friend's recovery after the attack the night before.

"I'm fine, Bess, thanks," Nancy replied. "I even went for my run this morning."

"Better you than me," Bess said with a grin. "I'd rather let my fingers do the running."

Then Ms. Hanson appeared, and the three of them rode the elevator upstairs together. Nancy explained Bess's presence in the office. "Nice to see you again, Bess," Ms. Hanson said warmly, shaking her hand. "I'm sure Nancy will be glad to have your help. That file-management work can be really tedious."

"Oh, I'm sure Nancy and I will find some way to make it interesting," Bess said, her blue eyes twinkling.

"Oh, I'm sure you and Nancy are interesting all by yourselves." A friendly male voice came from behind them. Henry Yi joined them with a flashing grin. "Good morning," he continued, sticking out his hand. "My name's Henry. What's yours?"

"Ah, the primo paralegal," Bess said, smiling.

"My reputation precedes me," Henry said. "I'm thrilled."

"My name's Bess Marvin," she went on. "I'm Nancy's friend, and I'll be working with her for the next few days."

"If your file management skills equal your poise and beauty, I'm afraid your work will be done all too soon," Henry said.

Bess rolled her eyes. "We'd better get started, Nan," she said, turning to her friend, "or I'll get fired before I even get hired."

"Your father and Blaine are in court this morning, Nancy," Ms. Hanson said. "And Byron's doing some research down there, so you two should have the library to yourselves."

"Great," Nancy said. "We'll get a lot done." The two girls moved off to the law library and set up at two adjacent computer stations. Nancy gave Bess a list of the cases, and they started copying files off

115

the computer system and onto floppy disks for storage.

Once the computers were up and running, Nancy reached into her portfolio and produced the disk she had found in the street the night before. Bess popped it in her disk drive.

The two girls looked carefully at the screen as Bess called up the directory. "Oh, my goodness," Nancy said, shocked. "These are all Blaine Warner's files."

"She must be the one who attacked you!" Bess cried.

13

Late-Night Stakeout

Nancy stared at the screen. "It's certainly a possibility that Blaine was the attacker," Nancy said. "I'm sure she'd be strong enough, and she's a bit taller than I am, too. But what's worse is these files are all about that new Harris case that Blaine and my dad are working on. Why was she carrying around a disk like that?"

"Maybe she was taking it home to work on. Do you think we should we give it back to her?" Bess asked, suddenly concerned. "What if Henry or Byron stole the disk from Blaine, and it fell out when one of them attacked you? Maybe Byron borrowed it and dropped it on his way to the Cyber Space. What if Blaine needs this disk to work on your father's case?"

"I'm sure she has the information stored on her hard drive as well," Nancy said. "Let's not tell anyone and see what happens."

"Okay, Nan," Bess said, exiting the directory and removing the disk, which Nancy slipped into her portfolio.

"Listen," Nancy continued softly, "I have an idea. Why don't you go ask Ms. Hanson if there's anything else you can do to help out around the office?"

"Sure," Bess said. "That way I can pop in and out of a few offices and snoop around a little." Bess stood up and walked out to the reception area, leaving the door to the library open. Nancy could hear Bess and Ms. Hanson's conversation.

"Hi, Ms. Hanson," Bess said. "Nancy suggested I ask if I can help out with anything else around the office—run errands, make phone calls, whatever you need."

Ms. Hanson smiled at her. "Why not?" she replied. "Here are some memos you can distribute to all the offices. And then maybe you can do a coffee run. I'd like a cheese Danish and a coffee with two sugars."

Nancy kept working in the library until Bess reappeared a few minutes later with a copy of the memo.

"Nancy, you'll never believe what happened," Bess said. "I walked into Blaine's office to give her a copy of the memo, and she was whispering into the

118

phone, something about erasing a file. I'll bet she tried to wipe out that E-mail log. And when she realized I was in there, she yelled at me to get out."

Before Nancy could ask her any questions, the girls heard a phone slam down across the hall, and Blaine burst in through the door to the law library. Ignoring Nancy and Bess, she started searching through the papers and disks on the table and shelves. She bent over to peer in the disk drives at each computer station.

"I just got back from court, and I discovered I'm missing a very important disk," Blaine stormed. She looked closely at Nancy and then at Bess. "Are you sure you didn't get it mixed up with those disks you've been copying?"

"No, Blaine," Nancy said carefully. "I'm sure I didn't get it mixed up with any of my disks."

"I was working late in the library last night, and I'm sure I left it in here. Unless Byron or Henry picked it up. Henry's always sticking his nose where it doesn't belong. And Byron's always snatching up disks and papers and stuffing them in his law books or his pockets. I'll bet one of them has it!" she huffed.

"Neither of them has been in here this morning. Didn't you say you were working late last night?" Nancy asked Blaine. "When would Byron or Henry have picked up your disk, if you were the last one in here?"

Blaine shot Nancy a hostile glance, then said,

"Maybe they took it during the day, and I didn't notice. They might even have taken it out of my office. No one ever knocks around here," she concluded, glaring at Bess as she stamped out of the library.

"Whew!" Bess exhaled. "And I thought she was upset before when I barged into her office."

"Well," Nancy said, her mind racing, "we know Byron couldn't have taken the disk last night, because he was at Art-Dot-Café—and the Cyber Space—at the same times we were."

"But it could have been Henry," Bess said. "Or maybe it *was* Byron, and he'd already passed the disk on to his partner in crime at Williams and Brown—and the accomplice is the one who attacked you and dropped the disk Byron had given him."

"I guess that's a possibility, too," Nancy replied. "But what's most likely is that Blaine was taking the disk home, and that she lied about working late last night. She probably realized that she must have dropped the disk when she attacked me. . . ."

"And now she's trying to cover it up, by trying to blame Byron or Henry," Bess concluded excitedly.

The girls quickly dropped their discussion as the library door opened, and Nancy's father walked in. "Hi, Bess; hi, Nancy," he said. "Sorry I missed you this morning. You two doing okay with that file copying?"

"Fine," Nancy said. "Bess has been helping Ms. Hanson distribute memos." Suddenly Nancy's computer made a *ping* sound, and she glanced at the screen. "Who's sending me E-mail?" she wondered aloud, and pressed a button to retrieve her mail.

There was a new message: "I'm in. Come hear me read—live and in person—tomorrow night at the Cyber Space. Please invite Bess.—Byron Thomas"

"Wow, I guess they liked his stuff," Bess said, reading over Nancy's shoulder.

"What's that?" Mr. Drew asked.

"Oh, we ran into Byron last night at a computer coffee bar in the warehouse district," Nancy explained to her father. "He wanted to arrange a poetry reading there, and I told him to E-mail me an invitation if he got the gig."

"I wonder where he's E-mailing you from," Bess said.

"He's probably on-line on the computers at the courthouse," Nancy's father answered her. "Blaine has him working down there today."

"So, what's up, Dad?" Nancy asked. "The last few days you've been too busy to stop in and say hello."

"I've got some more papers that have to go over to Williams and Brown," he replied. "I hate to pull you off your computer work again, but I figure with Bess helping out . . ."

"I'll go, Mr. Drew," Bess offered. "I was going on a coffee run anyway. I'll go to Williams and Brown first, and then pick up the food on my way back."

"Thanks, Bess," he said as he left the library. "And by the way, I take my coffee black, and I'd love a croissant."

Once he was gone, Nancy turned to her friend. "Listen, Bess, let's hide out in the office tonight and see if we can catch Blaine—or one of the others—stealing computer disks or sending out E-mail."

Bess grimaced. "Hey, I missed my on-line group last night, Nance. You want me to miss it again?"

"I really need you here," Nancy said. "The solution is right around the corner."

"No," Henry said, appearing in the doorway to the library. "*I'm* right around the corner. What are you two up to?" he asked.

"Nothing, Henry," Bess replied. "I was just going to deliver some papers for Mr. Drew and go on a coffee run for the office. Can I bring you something?"

"Hot tea and a scone, if you please, madame," he replied with his broad grin.

When Bess returned from Williams & Brown, she walked back into the library and gave Nancy her cup of tea and bagel. "I didn't turn up any new clues," Bess said. "How about you?" Nancy shook her head, and the two girls spent the rest of the day working quietly in the library.

A little after six o'clock, they gathered up their

things, shut off the computers, and walked out to the reception area.

"Good night, Ms. Hanson," Bess said.

"Good night, Bess, Nancy," Ms. Hanson said. "I'll be leaving in a few minutes. You girls aren't working late tonight?"

"No, we had enough for one day," Nancy said, laughing.

"Me, too," Ms. Hanson said. "I'll see you to-morrow."

Instead of getting on the elevator, the two girls went to the ladies' room at the end of the public hall. They saw Ms. Hanson turn out the lights in the reception area, set the automatic locks by the double glass doors, and get into the elevator. Once the doors had slid shut behind Ms. Hanson, Nancy entered the door-lock code, and the two girls sneaked quietly back into the office.

"Shh . . . I think I hear someone in the hallway," Nancy whispered. "Get in here." She pulled Bess into a small closet off the reception area.

"What is this?" Bess whispered.

"It's a utility closet," Nancy replied. "The fuse box, electrical panel, phone switches, and comput-er cables are all in here. I didn't want to go in the coat closet," she explained, "in case someone was leaving and wanted to get a coat."

Through the crack at the edge of the door, Nancy could see her father press a button next to the doors and wait a few seconds while the automatic lock disengaged. Then he exited the reception area doors to the elevator lobby.

"That was too close," Nancy said. "Let's take off our shoes, so when we go out we'll be really quiet."

Once Mr. Drew was gone, the two girls emerged from their hiding place and tiptoed up the hall toward the library in their stocking feet. They could see Blaine working at her desk by the light of a small desk lamp. The girls slipped into the dark silence of the law library. They hid underneath the long oak table housing the computer stations, concealed at the far end by the metal filing cabinets.

"Now what?" Bess whispered.

"Now we wait," Nancy whispered back.

They had a long wait. After nearly two hours, they heard the metallic click of the outer door.

"That must be Blaine leaving," Bess whispered. "I guess she's not doing anything tonight. Can we go now?"

"Shh," Nancy said. "That wasn't Blaine leaving. That was someone coming in!"

The door to the library opened softly, and a figure slipped into the darkened room. The girls saw Byron click on a small desk lamp, and power up one of the computers. He looked around nervously, slipped a disk out of his pocket and into the disk drive, and tapped away at the keyboard. The girls heard the telltale whine of a computer modem dialing out.

Then the overhead fluorescent lights came on.

Byron jumped out of his chair and turned off the computer.

"Byron," the two girls heard Blaine angrily say. "When did you come in? I've told you not to sneak around here at night and use our Internet link. What are you up to, anyway?"

"N-nothing, Ms. Warner," Byron said. "I just came back to enter these, um, notes. I didn't mean to startle you. I'm s-sorry."

"I'm leaving for the night," she said brusquely. "Did you check to make sure you didn't pick up my disk last night?"

"I left before you last night," Byron replied simply, "and I've been at the courthouse all day." He turned off the desk lamp and started for the door.

"I'm going to the ladies' room, and then I'm leaving," Blaine called out as she turned off the light and moved up the hallway. "I'll lock up when I'm done." The girls stayed hidden until they heard the outer door lock click shut.

"Great," Bess said. She wriggled out of her hiding place. "Everyone's gone home for the night. Our stakeout's a bust, and I can get home in time for my chat group."

"Wait a minute," Nancy whispered urgently. She reached out to grab Bess by the arm. "What about Henry?"

"Exactly." A deep male voice came from the darkened hallway. "What about Henry?"

Bess gave a little cry of surprise as the lights came on once again to reveal Henry standing in the doorway to the library.

"Henry!" Bess cried. "What are you doing here?"

"I might ask the same of you, but I already know the answer," he replied smugly. "You're here to help Nancy catch whoever sent that E-mail on those settled cases. But you're too late. I, Henry the Great, have figured it out," he whispered. "The E-mail mystery is solved, and the culprit is . . . Ms. Marian Hanson!"

14

The E-mail Trail

"What?" Nancy cried. "Ms. Hanson would never do anything to hurt my father, or help another firm—especially not Williams and Brown."

"Well, look at this," Henry said, waving a piece of paper at them. It was a printout of the E-mail log file that Nancy had discovered. "Her log-on is all over this E-mail that was sent to Williams and Brown on the same day the cases came into our office," Henry said triumphantly.

"Hold on just a minute, smart guy," Bess said. "That's the first thing I noticed, too. But you can pretend to be anyone you want in cyberspace, remember? You could have sent that, and just used Ms. Hanson's log-on name and password to cover your tracks."

"And you know everybody's password, Henry," Nancy said. "Remember when I forgot mine, and you told me what it was?"

"That's true," Henry admitted. "Your father insisted that we all have each other's passwords in case we need to access material in each other's files."

"You stick to the law, Mr. Hotshot Paralegal," Bess said, "and leave the investigating to us."

"I still think—" Henry began.

Nancy cut him off. "I think we should look at the disk that Byron forgot when Blaine surprised him here a few minutes ago to see if he's really the poet he claims to be—or if he's something else, altogether."

"Good idea, Nan," Bess said.

"I saw them both head out of the office," Henry said.

"You don't think they're working together?" Bess asked.

"No way," Henry replied. "Those two are like oil and water. They do not mix."

The three turned on the computer where Byron had been sitting and waited for it to boot up.

"Shh," Nancy whispered. "I think I hear something."

"Naw," Henry said. "That's just the computer warming up. So, what happened? Byron was sneaking in here to go on-line, and Blaine caught him?"

Nancy nodded, and once the computer screen showed it was ready, called up the first file on Byron's disk. Its contents scrolled down the screen.

> I dream in bits
> and bytes
> Of you
> My shining light
> My dream of day
> My unknown cyber love . . .

"Enough!" Henry said, rolling his eyes. "I've seen enough."

"I think it's beautiful," Bess said, glaring at Henry. "I've never seen a computer love poem before."

Nancy continued to scan the files, just to be sure, but it was all poetry or notes on Web-page design and memos to Internet writers' groups. It appeared that Byron was just what he claimed to be.

"Bess and I were pretty sure already," Nancy said thoughtfully. "But this confirms it. If your interest in these settled cases is for real, and if Byron's activities on-line are truly about his poetry, then Blaine's our main suspect."

"And she might be dangerous," Bess warned. "Nancy was attacked last night, outside the Cyber Space Café—and we found Blaine's missing disk right there, where she was attacked."

"Blaine's missing disk?" Henry exclaimed. "She's been screaming about that all day. Let's take a look at it."

"We already did," Nancy said. "There's nothing on it but files from the Harris case."

"She shouldn't be taking that out of the office anyway," Henry said. "That material is highly confidential and very important to the case. Boy, this really does make it look like Blaine's the one behind all this. Sorry I ever doubted you, Ms. Hanson," he called out to the empty reception area.

"Well, Mr. Know-it-all, do you know Blaine's log-on password?" Bess asked.

"Of course I do," Henry replied.

"Then let's go into her office and have a look at her private files," Nancy said. "We need solid proof that she's the one who's been sending information to Williams and Brown."

The trio turned off the computer and the lights in the library, and walked across the hall to Blaine's office. There they switched on her small desk lamp and computer, and waited for it to warm up.

When the screen prompt glowed, Henry entered Blaine's log-on password, and they started to scan all the files and directories relating to E-mail, file transfers, and communications.

"She's got Williams and Brown's E-mail address on her modem address book," Henry pointed out.

"That's not necessarily suspicious," Nancy said. Her eyes darted over the information on the screen. "She could have that for legitimate purposes. What else is there?"

Henry started pulling floppy disks out of Blaine's storage file and feeding them into the disk drive one after the other. "Why would Blaine do something like this?" he asked.

"She went to Walker Law with John Brown Junior of Williams and Brown," Nancy said. "And they do know each other. I saw them having lunch together at the deli yesterday. Maybe he's paying her to get him information he can use to settle these cases, save money for Williams and Brown's clients, and impress his father."

"Does he have curly brown hair?" Bess asked.

"He sure does," Nancy replied.

"Then he was with Blaine when we saw them at the Sacred Cow the other night," Bess added excitedly. "I saw him at Williams and Brown today when I delivered those papers for your dad. I knew I'd seen him before."

"But this is all just speculation," Nancy said. "I need hard evidence."

"What's this?" Bess interrupted, pointing at something far down on the list of files in the directory of the last disk Henry had fed into the drive.

"It says 'phone bills,'" Henry read aloud.

"But everything else in this directory is legal files and case notes and office correspondence," Nancy noted. "Why is there a file of phone bills in here?"

"Let's take a look," Henry said, opening up the file labeled "phone bills."

And there, in the mislabeled file, were personal background notes on all the clients who had settled early.

"Look at this," Nancy whispered. "This information comes from their old criminal case files. I remember some of this from when I read through the records in storage. Bob Jamison's old injury, Jeannette King's false theft charge, Harriet Wasser's indictment for withholding heat from her tenants. This is all information that they'd want kept quiet."

"Wow, Councilman Fox had a drunk-driving conviction?" Henry exclaimed. "Mister Get-Tough-on-Crime? No wonder he settled fast. He wouldn't want that to be made public, especially not right now, when he's running for mayor."

"And look at the bottom of this file," Bess said. "It's a list of dollar amounts and dates. I'll bet that's what John Brown Junior paid her for sending him this information."

"This proves it, all right," Nancy said. "This information could definitely have been used to pressure those clients into accepting early settlements."

"But how can we prove she's been working with

John Brown?" Bess asked. "That E-mail log file just shows Williams and Brown as the destination phone number. It doesn't give any receiver names."

"That log file shows only the information covered in our communications program," Henry explained. "Like the fact that MHans made the transmission." He shook his head. "I can't believe I fell for that. Blaine must have changed her screen name in our in-house E-mail logs."

"I knew Ms. Hanson wouldn't do this," Nancy said. "And look at the transmission times. They're too late at night for her."

"We need the base information stored in the mail server," Henry said. "Give me some dates," he said, his fingers flying over the keyboard.

The two girls watched in fascination as the screen filled with letters, numbers, names, dates, abbreviations.

"What is all that?" Nancy asked, mystified.

"Most mail programs filter out all this stuff," Henry said. "But it's what tells the mail server how to route the mail, identifies each computer user who sends E-mail out, and where it went. Take a look." He pointed to what looked to Nancy like a coded language.

From BWarn@drew.com Fri May 22 19:26:03 1998
Received: from drew.com by willbr.com with SMTP (1.39.205.11.15.3) id AA21901

(4.1/SMI for johnjr@willbr.com); Fri 22
    May 1998 19:29:05 -0400
Date: Fri 22 May 9819:29:05 -0400
From: Blaine Warner <BWarn@drew.com>
To: John Brown Jr. <johnjr@willbr.com>
Subject: Phone bills

"You see?" Henry said. "The original transmission shows it was sent from Blaine's computer after nine o'clock at night," Henry said. "You have to know an awful lot to cover your tracks on a computer."

"Now we've got the proof we need," Nancy said. "It's time to call my father and tell him that his new associate has been up to no good."

Nancy picked up the phone and dialed her home number. While she waited for her father to pick up, Henry and Bess read through more of the material in Blaine's secret mislabeled file.

Mr. Drew answered. "Hello?"

"Hi, Dad," Nancy said. "Bess and I are still in the office."

"I wondered where you were," he said. "Ms. Hanson told me you left before me. Hannah was starting to get worried when you didn't come home. Did something come up at the office?"

"Yes, Dad. Something serious. We just discovered files in Blaine Warner's computer disks that strongly indicate she sent privileged information from the old criminal cases of those clients who recently settled their cases."

"What?" Mr. Drew said, shocked.

"There's a summary of notes from the old cases, with either compromising or delicate information," Nancy went on. "And there's also a list of dollar amounts and dates that seem to show she was paid for getting this information."

"I can't believe this happened in my office," Mr. Drew said. "How did you find out about it?"

"Henry was suspicious, too. That's why he made that list I told you about. He helped us get into Blaine's computer system, and then he went into the mail server information, where we discovered Blaine had sent E-mail to John Brown Junior at Williams and Brown."

"This is serious, Nan—"

Before her father could say anything more, the phone went dead, the computer screen went black, and the entire office was plunged into darkness.

135

15

An Inside Job

Bess screamed. Nancy and Henry shushed her.

"Be quiet, Bess," Nancy said firmly. "Blaine must have come back. I'll bet that was the noise I heard before."

"She must have overheard everything," Henry whispered. "We've got to try to stop her from getting away."

"I can find my way around here, even in the dark," Nancy continued in a whisper. "Follow me."

They all held hands, and Nancy led them silently around Blaine's desk and through the door. They walked up the darkened hallway to the darkened reception area.

Some light from the elevator area shone in

through the thick double glass doors. Bess whispered, "I'll wait here and stand guard. You guys go ahead and get the lights turned back on."

"Okay, Bess," Nancy said, still holding on to Henry. "We'll be right back. Don't let Blaine get out." Nancy steered Henry carefully into the small utility closet off the reception area, where the electrical panel was located.

"I can't see a thing," Henry said.

"Here," Nancy said. "I keep a penlight on my keychain." She held the button at the tip of the flashlight that looked like a ballpoint pen, and a faint beam of light shone onto switches and wires in the electrical panel.

"Someone's thrown off the main power switch," Henry said, looking closely. "I've just got to turn it back on and—"

Before they could do anything, they heard a scuffle. Bess screamed and cried, "She's out here!"

Quickly Henry and Nancy turned the main power switch back on, and ran out into the reception area to find Blaine Warner holding a silver award cup over Bess's head, about to hit her!

"Stop!" Nancy called.

Blaine turned around, clearly startled. Bess tried to jump away. Blaine grabbed her by the arm, and Bess shrieked again.

"Let me go," Bess cried, struggling with the tall, angry woman.

"Let her go!" Nancy echoed her friend.

137

Blaine froze and eyed Nancy with hatred. "You!" Blaine snarled. "I thought I'd scared you off at the Cyber Space last night. I heard you at the restaurant when you planned to go on-line with your little friend here and look for help tracking E-mail."

"You *are* SEEK!" Bess gasped. "And you're the one who attacked Nancy last night." She tried to pull away, but Blaine's grip was too tight.

Blaine laughed. "Yeah, I sent you that note about the rose. I thought that would grab you, Little Miss Romance. And I set up the meeting when you'd have to run off to your precious chat group, so Nancy would be all alone."

She turned to Nancy. "I thought I'd be able to get you out of the way for good."

"We found the floppy disk with the file you called 'phone bills,'" Nancy said.

"Your father's always bragging about what a super-sleuth his daughter is," Blaine went on. "I was worried you might figure out my scheme. Henry here couldn't find his brains without a map."

Nancy heard a sharp intake of breath from Henry, and then he said, "You fooled me with Ms. Hanson's password, Blaine. But we found the original E-mail information, and we know what you and John Brown Junior have been doing."

"Good for you," Blaine snapped. "Now you've got to catch me. I'm out of here, and you can't stop me." She shoved Bess away from her forcefully, and Bess fell over the low coffee table. She scattered the magazines to the floor and moaned.

"Bess!" Nancy cried. She ran over to her friend. Henry followed close behind.

Blaine took advantage of the moment and headed for the office door. With one hand, she pressed the button for the automatic lock. With the other, she threw the heavy cup behind her.

Bess and Nancy were protected behind the low coffee table, but the heavy cup struck Henry in the leg, and he stumbled, groaning in pain. Bess screamed again.

"Henry, are you okay?" Bess asked.

"Never mind me, just stop her," he said, holding his leg. Nancy was sure he'd been injured pretty badly. The cup itself was heavy, and it was mounted on a large wooden base with sharp edges.

"All right, Henry. Call the police and an ambulance, too. Come on, Bess," Nancy said. "Can you walk?"

Bess nodded. Though still shaken up from her fall, Bess joined her friend.

The heavy glass office doors had locked automatically after Blaine's exit, and by the time the girls buzzed themselves out, the elevator door had closed behind Blaine, and she was gone.

"Oh, no!" Bess exclaimed.

"The stairs," Nancy cried, and they headed for the fire stairs.

"Four flights," Bess groaned, panting a little after her recent ordeal. They rushed down the stairs, only to see Blaine exit the building and run into the street. "She's going to get away," Bess cried.

"No, she's not," Nancy said. "Look."

Right outside the office building was a police car, lights flashing and sirens wailing. Mr. Drew was pulling up behind it in his sedan.

"There she is, officers," Nancy cried, pointing to Blaine Warner.

Mr. Drew rushed over to Nancy and Bess. "Are you two all right?" he asked. "When the phone was cut off while you were telling me about the conspiracy between Blaine and John Brown Junior, I thought the worst. So I called the police and rushed over as quickly as I could. I'm afraid I may have broken a few traffic rules on the way."

"I'm glad you got here so fast," Nancy replied. She gave her father a hug. "I'm fine."

"Blaine knocked me down," Bess said breathlessly. "I'm okay, but I'm afraid Henry may be really hurt. She threw that big award cup at us, and it caught him in the leg."

"Where is he?" Nancy's father asked.

"We left him upstairs in the reception area," Nancy answered. "We didn't want to let Blaine get away, so when we missed the elevator we ran down the stairs."

"Four flights," Bess said again with a groan. "With his leg hurt, Henry really couldn't keep up,"

Bess added. "But he was going to call the police and an ambulance."

Just then Henry appeared in the doorway to the office building, limping. "The police got here really fast," he said.

Nancy smiled at him. "My father called them when our call got cut off."

"Good thing," Henry said. He flashed his famous grin, a little wearily. "I called an ambulance, too. I ought to get this dent in my leg checked out. It hurts a lot. At the very least, it's going to be purple by tomorrow. Did you catch Blaine?" he asked, wincing.

"Yes," Bess said. "She's right over there with the men in blue. Let me help you over to that bench, so you can sit down." Bess put her shoulder under Henry's arm.

Nancy and Mr. Drew walked over as the police took Blaine Warner into custody. "What's the charge, Mr. Drew?" the officer asked.

"How about assault with a deadly award cup?" Henry called out, his face pale.

"This is industrial espionage, Blaine," Mr. Drew said gravely. "You stole information from my firm. This is a criminal matter, so you will be prosecuted as a thief. And if you or John Brown Junior used privileged information to threaten my clients, or coerce them into taking settlements—in fact, if you had any contact with them whatsoever—you will both be disbarred."

"John will post bail for me before sunrise," she retorted. "And you'll have to prove the rest of it in court."

"We have all the proof we need," Nancy said, looking straight at Blaine.

"Oh, right. Miss Junior Detective here is going to testify against me in court," Blaine said sarcastically. "Well, Williams and Brown will back me up all the way. After all I've done for them, it's the least they can do for me."

"Remember, miss," one of the police officers said. "Anything you say can be used against you in a court of law."

"I know that, you fool," Blaine snapped. "I'm a lawyer."

As the police led Blaine away, Nancy asked her father, "What are you going to do, Dad? Can you still help the clients who were scared into accepting those settlements?"

"I'm afraid it's too late for that," he replied, "but I'm going to bring a suit against Blaine and John Brown Junior for theft and fraud. Maybe we can put together a class-action suit against them as well. At the very least, they're going to be disbarred. They might even go to jail. And despite Ms. Warner's wishes, I'm afraid Williams and Brown won't be able to back her up at all, or their firm will be destroyed. This will rock their reputation as it is."

Mr. Drew looked at the three young people and

said, "Nancy, you can fill me in on this case—on our way to the hospital. We need to make sure Henry and Bess here weren't injured too badly.

"Honestly, Nancy," he added with a grin, "you sure know how to make a summer temp job interesting."

16

Summer Vacation—At Last!

The next day at the office Ms. Hanson, Henry, Byron, and Mr. Drew gathered to discuss the case with Nancy and Bess. Henry's leg was in a cast, and he leaned jauntily on his crutches.

"How did you figure out what Blaine was doing?" Ms. Hanson asked.

"A lot of it was just plain luck," Nancy said. "My father had expressed his concern about these cases settling so early. And I knew something was up when I found that E-mail log file and saw that the dates on those transmissions were on the same days the cases were first received," she explained. "And then I overheard some conversations at Williams and Brown that gave me a possible motive. When I called Bess to ask for her help in tracing the E-mail,

Blaine must have been eavesdropping and heard us plan to meet at the Sacred Cow restaurant."

"Then Blaine and John Brown Junior sat behind us, and overheard us plan to go on-line and look for a computer expert," Bess continued. "So when I posted a note on the local computer users' bulletin board, Blaine left us a reply that same night, pretending to be a computer expert called SEEK."

"SEEK. So that's what you were talking about at the Cyber Space that night," Byron said.

"You didn't help matters, always sneaking on-line to do your poetry stuff," Nancy said.

Bess turned to Byron. "You know, you left a disk with one of your poems on it in the library last night. I really liked it."

"You did?" Byron said, blushing and smiling at Bess. "Well, you and Nancy have to come to my poetry reading at the Cyber Space tonight. Everybody else, too." He added, after a pause, "Did you guys really suspect me?"

"Both you and Henry were suspects for a while," Nancy admitted.

"I know, I know," Henry said. "Finding that list of the clients I wrote down must have made you suspicious. But I was suspicious, too. I just wanted to figure out what was going on here."

"Which I appreciate," Mr. Drew said, smiling at his paralegal.

"And we wouldn't have gotten the proof we

needed if it weren't for your computer expertise," Nancy said generously.

"Yeah," Henry said, grimacing, "but if you hadn't pointed me in the right direction I would've done just what Blaine wanted, and blamed Ms. Hanson for everything."

"Henry, how could you think I'd do anything like that?" Ms. Hanson asked. "I must say, I'm a bit surprised and hurt."

"I'm sorry," Henry said. "I just followed the clues I found. I didn't think about the fact that you can use someone else's password and log-on. And I'm supposed to be the computer whiz around here." He looked at Bess and Nancy and blushed slightly. "If it weren't for Nancy and Bess, I wouldn't have figured anything out."

"So after Blaine left you this note, pretending to be a computer expert called SEEK, then what happened?" Ms. Hanson asked.

"We had an on-line chat with SEEK," Bess explained, "and arranged to meet at the Cyber Space Café."

"Blaine must have been on-line as SEEK in her own office, while we were in the library," Nancy said.

"That's kind of creepy," Mr. Drew said. "This whole thing is like a spy movie."

"I've learned a lot about the Internet from this case," Nancy went on. "On-line, you can pretend to be anyone—and any*where*."

"So the next night," Bess continued, "when Nancy and I went to meet SEEK at the Cyber Space, I had to run home for my on-line chat group, and when Nancy left the café alone, Blaine attacked her."

"You should have told me what was going on then," Nancy's father scolded. "You could have been in real danger."

"I told you about my suspicions," Nancy said. "But I needed proof. I had to show a solid connection between someone here and someone at Williams and Brown before I did anything. Anyway, when she jumped me, Blaine dropped a disk she was carrying with files from the Harris case. That made us pretty sure it was her, but we decided to stake out the office the next day to see if we could catch her in the act."

"But I caught you in the act, instead," Henry said with a grin.

"And it's a good thing you did," Bess said. "We all worked together and found the notes from the old case files and the mail-server information, which proves that Blaine was E-mailing John Brown Junior at Williams and Brown."

"Their reputation's going to suffer for this kind of illegal activity, you can bet on it," Ms. Hanson said. "I don't care if they claim they didn't know what John Brown Junior was up to. They profited from his and Blaine's scheme."

"That doesn't help us," Henry said. "Mr. Drew

147

doesn't handle the kind of insurance cases they do."

"I'm not going after Williams and Brown for their business," Mr. Drew said. "I've got enough of my own. And I don't have anything against the firm—just John Brown Junior for doing illegal things to advance his own career. We'll get Blaine's banking records and follow the money trail."

"You can match up deposits with the dates and dollar amounts we found on that disk in Blaine's office," Nancy said. "I'm just glad it's all over. I'm really looking forward to going sailing with George."

"I think I'll invite myself along, if that's okay," Bess said.

"Fine with me," Nancy said.

"Good," Bess replied. "I deserve a little R and R at sea. Sailing isn't hard work, is it?" she added, smiling at her friend.

"Not at all," Byron said, gazing at Bess. "It's very romantic."

"Send me a poem while I'm away," Bess said with a grin.

"You'd make a good lawyer," Henry said to Nancy. "A lot of legal research is just snooping around."

"I prefer to call it investigating," Nancy said. She and Bess laughed together, and the others joined in.

NANCY DREW® MYSTERY STORIES By Carolyn Keene

A MINSTREL BOOK
Published by Pocket Books

THE HARDY BOYS® SERIES By Franklin W. Dixon

Sometimes, it takes a kid to solve a good crime....

Original stories based on the hit Nickelodeon show!

To find out more about *The Mystery Files of Shelby Woo* or any other Nickelodeon show, visit Nickelodeon Online on America Online (Keyword: NICK) and on the Web at www.nick.com.

A MINSTREL® BOOK
Published by Pocket Books

1338-05